W9-BKW-672

PRIM AND IMPROPER

Rachel Vincer

A KISMET® Romance

METEOR PUBLISHING CORPORATION
Bensalem, Pennsylvania

First Printing May 1993.

ISBN: 1-56597-061-6

Printed in the United States of America.

RACHEL VINCER

Rachel Vincer confesses to being an unregenerate romantic who loves music, reading and traveling to exotic places looking for stories and inspiration. After a childhood spent in India and England, she now makes her home in Toronto, but considers the world her oyster.

Other books by Rachel Vincer:

No. 117 *HOT COPY*

ONE

"I can put up with your bad imitations of Queen Elizabeth. Occasionally I might enjoy your incessant whistling. And I don't even mind those smelly fish sandwiches . . ."

"Kippers, please." Martin could barely restrain his laughter. Could that actually be anger hardening Julia Bennett's soft voice as she stood on the opposite side of their editor's office? He couldn't believe what he was seeing. What had happened? He'd finally cracked the facade of the ice maiden.

"I don't care what they are," Julia gave him an impatient look. "The point is . . ."

"Yes, what exactly is your point, Bennett?" He was beginning to enjoy himself. Maybe, finally, they were going to get things out in the open. Her cool disdain got under his skin so much it was driving him crazy.

A tiny shudder rippled down her spine as she forced herself to hold the penetrating gaze of the lean, bearded man lounging on the broad windowsill, framed by the wintry Toronto skyline.

She didn't relish confrontations, and with Martin Taylor in particular. He seemed to take a fiendish delight in raising her hackles. She took a deep breath, forcing herself to remain cool. *When you lose your temper, Julia, you lose control,* the major's gruff voice echoed in her head. But hadn't her father also taught her to stand up for herself?

"The point *is* that I won't let you steal one more story out from under my nose." No matter how hard she tried to keep her tone calm, she could hear the telltale tremble in her voice. She couldn't let him see how much he got to her.

Below the unruly mop of sun-streaked blond hair, a hint of world-weariness darkened Martin's blue eyes—the only sign he'd even noticed her emotional turmoil. And she knew very well that he'd noticed.

"Hey," he shrugged his broad shoulders, "you snooze, you lose." His soft English accent took none of the sting from the heartless gibe, tossed off so casually, but his eyes held hers, keen and watchful, as if gauging her reaction.

Give me a gun and I'll shoot this man. Julia let out her breath through clenched teeth and turned to her editor.

Roger Dubois had said barely a word since she walked into his seventh-floor office and found her nemesis perched on the windowsill. Chair swiveled slightly toward the window, the editor sat behind his desk, bulldog face sunk in an impenetrable silence, following the exchange of words with his eyes as if it were a tennis match.

"Roger? . . ." she urged. *Come on. Step in. Tell Martin hands off.* After all, her editor was the one who gave her the story in the first place.

He leaned farther back in the old black leather chair, slowly stroking one temple with his index finger, and regarded her with a mixture of surprise and amusement. His only response was an imperceptible lift of his shaggy eyebrows.

"Look, Roger, you promised me this would be my first cover story. But for two months now, *he*," she flung a finger in the direction of the bearded vulture perched against the corner of the plate glass. "*He* has swiped every important article to come along since he set foot in this building." Unperturbed, Martin sat with one long leg drawn up on the sill, swinging the other carelessly back and forth.

"Julia . . ." Roger slowly shook his head and turned slightly toward the window. Martin caught his gaze, leaning an elbow on the well-worn knee of his tan corduroy trousers to rest his bearded chin on his fist. A silent message passed between the two men.

What was this, a conspiracy? She wasn't given to paranoia, but she was starting to wonder.

Julia dragged her gaze back to Roger. "This is the fourth time you've suggested an assignment to me and I've gone ahead with the preliminary research, then you've turned around and handed it to him . . ."

"You're breaking my heart," Martin's precise voice cut in as he slipped off the windowsill and sauntered around in front of the desk.

Grabbing an armless office chair, he straddled it casually, folding his arms along the back. His gaze slid over to the other man with a mocking shrug, with the clear implication that they'd better humor this poor martyr.

Julia took a deep, shaky breath. What would they do if she gave in to the impulse to jump up on Roger's desk and scream, "I'm sick and tired and I'm not going to take it anymore"? That would wipe that smug, superior look off Martin Taylor's face. Just imagining it gave her a certain vicarious satisfaction.

"As I was saying," she continued evenly, "when you gave me this assignment, I thought I was finally getting somewhere. That you believed I was ready. And I am. Now I'm counting on you to do the right thing."

Julia aimed a beseeching look at Roger, willing him to be fair. He and Martin had known each other since their days as war correspondents covering the turmoil in Beirut, but Roger had shown his old friend enough favoritism. Surely he must be aware of the grumbling from other members of the staff who'd had their toes stepped on, too.

After all, the man had blown into *Canadian Horizons* like Hurricane Martin, with his cosmopolitan experience and hard-nosed tactics, and proceeded to shake up the calm, civilized atmosphere. He might be an excellent journalist, but she had wondered more than once what brought him to a modest human-interest magazine, worlds removed from *Newsweek* or *Paris Match,* or any of the more prestigious employers he claimed to have worked for.

Roger cleared his throat, his brusque voice sounding almost conciliatory for once. "You know, Julia, you don't really have the same level of experience."

Darting a glance at Martin, she found him still eyeing her with unsettling intensity, making her turn quickly back to Roger.

"Well, of course I don't. I'd be the first to admit that. But how will I get the experience unless you give me the chance to prove myself?" She placed a palm on the desk and leaned slightly toward the editor. "I can do a good job. Just let me try."

In reply Roger swiveled his chair slightly toward the window and studied the icy dockside seven floors below. Watching his stocky profile, Julia felt weighed down by apprehension.

"You forgot, 'Please, sir, I want some more, sir.' "

Martin's patronizing voice made her stiffen and straighten up, drawing her attention back to the man on the other side of the desk. Not that she'd been unaware of him for a second. How she wished he'd stop watching her, like a hungry wolf eyeing an unprotected lamb.

It took an effort to keep her voice even. "You may find all this very amusing, but this is my career we're talking about. I happen to take it very seriously."

"Excuse me, Bennett," Martin Taylor drew out her name in his husky voice, the English accent more pronounced in his scornful drawl. "If you can restrain your virtuous outrage for a moment. I'll have you know this story idea was mine from the start."

His idea! She hesitated for a moment, then looked across the large messy desk to Roger, apparently still fascinated by the gray expanse of Lake Ontario. But this could change everything! It might be done all the time, and she wouldn't put it past Martin, but she would never steal another journalist's idea.

"Is this true? *Is* it his idea? You told me it was yours."

Roger shook his head. "Did I? I can't remember."

What was going on here? It wasn't like Roger to be so evasive. She felt her heart sink.

"Allow me to refresh your memory," Martin cut in. "Does an evening at The Porkers Stern ring a bell?"

Julia rolled her eyes. Right about now that's exactly where she'd like to consign him. She folded her arms across the jacket of her trim navy suit and shifted her weight, tapping the toe of her high-heeled pump on the carpet.

Martin slanted her a sideways look. "Naturally someone with your social standing wouldn't be caught dead in such an inferior establishment."

She tried to ignore the disdainful dig. He considered her a snob; she'd got that message plainly enough a month ago. And all because she'd refused a few invitations to join the crowd from work at the nearby English pub.

But Brian always had other plans for them, much as she would have liked to go. Dinners with clients, charity functions where he hoped to rub elbows with the influential and advance his legal career. Brian was the one who wouldn't be caught dead in an unpretentious pub. In the weeks since they'd gone their separate ways, it had appalled Julia to realize how she'd allowed him to run her social life.

"They were running an item on the news channel about some mysterious remains from the War of 1812 dug up on a construction site in Niagara," Martin continued, his voice clipped and businesslike, "and I distinctly recall coming up with the idea for an article almost exactly like the one Bennett here is working on. *I'm* the one who suggested using the discovery as a hook and tying in some background about the events of the war in the region."

Roger shifted his tall, bulky frame in the chair and glared. "Yeah . . . yeah. I remember." He sounded bored and impatient, as if he'd had enough.

Julia opened her mouth to speak, but he held up his hand and turned to Martin.

"Okay, so you came up with the idea." He glanced back at Julia. "And you've been waiting to do a cover. So here's what we'll do." He paused and Julia leaned forward a fraction. Once again she saw a resurgence of sly amusement as his gaze went from one to the other. "You work together on this."

"Collaborate?" she gasped, but Martin made it sound more like a four-letter word as he surged to his feet and pushed the chair aside.

Julia flinched at his unexpected movement. It brought his tightly knit, six-foot frame close enough for her to detect the faint, subtle fragrance of cologne.

"You've got to be kidding." The prospect filled her with dismay.

"I don't want to hear another word on this. If you have anything else to say, say it to each other. I want this story on my desk in two weeks." Roger gave them both a look that dared them to argue.

Julia knew better than that, but the prospect appalled her. Still, half a story was better than none. Her eyes slid back to Martin, and she noticed his face tightening, an angry flush of color on his cheekbones.

"I've slotted the story for the May cover," Roger added. "Focus on Niagara-on-the-Lake and maybe we'll pick up some more advertising from the Shaw Festival. Now good-bye."

How often had she read the phrase *her blood chilled* and thought it was a ludicrous exaggeration? But now she knew exactly what that meant as she caught the anger in Martin's eyes. An icy shiver rippled down her spine, and a million tiny goose bumps came up all over her skin. She had fought so hard to ride the tiger, but now that she had succeeded it looked like a very dangerous perch. Perhaps if she were smart, she'd just toss the story right back to him.

With studied indolence, Martin bent to pick up his battered khaki knapsack from the floor beside the chair and slung it over one shoulder. He ambled over to the door and threw her a mocking glance. "So, Bennett, shall we head down there tomorrow?"

His swift change of mood made her pause with a slight frown of suspicion. "Yes, all right . . . the sooner, the better."

"Good. Then you can pick me up at nine. I'll give you my address."

Aside from his breathtaking nerve, she didn't like that dangerous gleam in his eye one bit. "Hold on a minute. I don't mind giving you a ride, but you could at least ask me."

"Look, Bennett, you're going to have to learn to get off that high horse of yours."

Julia took a deep breath. She wouldn't let him draw her into another argument. "Fine," she said with elaborate patience. "Why don't you just leave your address on my desk. But it'll have to be later. I have work to finish off tomorrow morning."

Beneath the short beard, his mouth curved into a smile that was downright satanic. Suddenly all the ramifications of collaboration came home to her. Cooped up with him in her small Escort for an hour and a half? Spending the next two weeks working together? How could she cope with a man who'd never even used her first name?

"We'll get together and discuss the plans later, shall we?"

She could tell by the insinuating tone in his voice and the twinkle in his eyes that he was relishing her discomfort. This man was going to do everything he could to punish her for sticking to her guns, she just knew it. Well, let him throw his worst at her, she could handle it.

Julia squared her shoulders. "Yes, why don't we do that," she said, pleased by the confident sound of her own voice. She wouldn't cave in under pressure and she'd do a good job to boot.

The door closed behind him and she watched his loose-limbed stride as he strolled past the office window, his lips pursed in a whistle. He stopped to flash a dazzling smile at Eunice, Roger's middle-aged secretary, and be rewarded with a delighted grin.

Julia shook her head. With his long, untidy blond hair and the darker gold whiskers obscuring his face, Martin looked as though he'd just walked out of the bush—an impression his rough and ready wardrobe tended to confirm. He certainly didn't have the kind of looks that appealed to her. But she was well aware not everyone shared her opinion. His English accent and raffish, worldly manner had bowled over more than a few women in the office. Like him or not, he had the kind of undeniable presence that made the air fairly crackle around him. He wasn't a man to inspire lukewarm feelings.

When it suited him, he could be very engaging and she had no doubt he wouldn't hesitate to use that talent to get what he wanted. Personally, she found it difficult to be charmed while he was devastating her professional pride. Julia scooped up her three-page outline from the desk with hands that still trembled a little.

Roger leaned back in his chair until the springs squeaked, and he rubbed his late-day stubble. "You might not think so now, but I'm doing you a favor."

She bit back the urge to be sarcastic and confined herself to a polite, "Oh?"

"You want to know why you haven't done a cover yet? Because I've had my doubts about whether you're tough enough for the job."

"But Roger . . ."

"However . . ." He held up his hand. "I like the way you stood up for yourself. I'm giving you a chance here. Don't blow it. Martin's quite capable of handling this by himself. I did this for you. So you'd get a chance to learn from a real pro."

She couldn't say a word, just stared at him. His casual dismissal of two years' hard work at the magazine left her too stunned to react. If she'd suspected beforehand how little faith Roger had in her ability, she would never have had the guts to storm into his office. Well, she was just going to have to show him he was wrong.

His heavy jowled face seemed to soften a little. He sighed. "It's too bad you two don't get along. Martin's a great guy. You could learn a lot from him."

"Look, I had a completely open mind before he came. I welcomed the idea of working with a journalist who had so much experience, until I met him."

How well she remembered his first week. He seemed to spend all his time either holding people in thrall with highly colored stories of his foreign exploits or telling them how to run the magazine better. Her enthusiasm had waned rapidly.

Roger swiveled his chair to the computer beside his desk and flicked it on. "I know he can be a real pain when he wants to be, but that's what makes a good reporter out in the field. Someone who doesn't let anything stand between him and the story."

Julia paused halfway to the door. "Does that include people, too, Roger?"

He gave a cynical chuckle. "That's your problem. You're too soft."

"Yes," she murmured, "I'm beginning to see that I have been."

"The point is we need Martin," he continued, his voice more brisk. "This isn't common knowledge, but he came up here as a personal favor to me. I knew he was looking for a change from New York, and I asked him to help us raise the profile of the magazine. You must have known we were in financial trouble."

A year ago, when Roger took over as managing editor, she'd heard rumors that circulation and ad revenues had been dropping but had never dreamed the problems were as serious as his grave face suggested. She felt the slightest twinge of hurt that Roger didn't have enough faith in the existing staff to put things right.

"I wanted him to guarantee me twelve months here, but he won't go beyond ten. Luckily for me, he'd never been to Canada and wanted to see the country, but I had to promise him enough interesting features to keep him challenged and occupied. I'm sorry if you've felt shafted, but we need him. I have to keep him happy."

Julia clutched the papers tighter, feeling as though a switch had been turned on in her head. What a relief to know it hadn't been her imagination or, worse yet, a budding persecution complex.

The hum of electronic machinery and babble of voices met her ears as she hurried out of Roger's sanctum into the organized chaos of the outer office.

His revelation made her see the situation in a rather different light. For the sake of the magazine, and her own career, she should do everything in her power to make this assignment run smoothly. Perhaps frustration and wounded pride had made her oversensitive where Martin was concerned. But Roger was right about one thing. She still had plenty to learn, and if she were smart, she'd grab this opportunity with both hands.

At the end of the hall Julia paused and attempted to knock on the cushioned partition enclosing Martin's office, then poked her head around the corner. The black lugged soles of his hiking boots met her eyes as he sat with his feet up on the desk, talking on the phone. From the soft warmth in his voice she sensed it wasn't a business call.

"I'll come back," she murmured, embarrassed for some reason she couldn't fathom, but he shook his head and motioned her to sit down. She settled in the chair in front of his desk, feeling decidedly strange. It must have been because she'd never been in his office before, much less talked to him, one on one.

"How about if I come down and meet you after work . . . all right, shall we say five o'clock?" Martin hung up and leaned back.

There she sat, cold as ice in her perfect suit with her perfect hair. My God, even her skin was perfect. It gave him a sour satisfaction knowing that he'd finally riled her in Roger's office, but that frosty reserve was back in place and as impenetrable as ever. It drove him crazy and he just wished he could understand why.

"To what do I owe the honor of this unprecedented visit, Bennett?"

"I do have a first name. Why don't you use it?"

He could tell the exasperated words had tumbled out unintentionally. She made a visible effort to get herself under control. Just for once he'd like to see her really lose it.

Julia took a deep breath. "Look, we have to work together. It would be much easier if we made a stab at getting along."

He laced his hands behind his head and regarded her for a moment. He'd better watch it. He was getting obsessive about this whole thing. "It's a novel concept, but I'm game."

The cool amusement in his blue eyes made her feel as if he were toying with her, seeing how far he could push her. How was she ever going to keep her composure when he refused to take her seriously?

Julia forced herself to assume a calm, reasonable tone. "Good. So what's your plan for this collaboration?"

He held her gaze for a long time, so long she thought he wasn't going to answer. Muffled by the partitions, the office noises seemed suddenly miles away. She felt acutely conscious of being alone with him for the first time, ever, and of the power his eyes held to disturb her. So much more disturbing, now their compelling intensity was undiluted by distractions. A clear, unruffled blue, they locked with hers in a scrutiny so penetrating she felt exposed and deeply vulnerable. As if he could see into her soul and read her deepest secrets. It was crazy, but it took an act of will to keep herself from bolting.

Swinging his feet to the floor with a thud, he came around the desk and leaned against the corner less than two feet away. He stood so close she had to crane her neck in order to lift her gaze from his lean corduroy-clad hips, all the way up the bulky cream sweater, to the shrewd gleam in his narrowed eyes. The silence pulled even tighter, so that she felt relieved when he finally spoke.

"I've got another suggestion. But I don't think you've got the guts to do it," he said casually.

She didn't miss the sly sideways look. He was baiting her again, but in spite of herself, she couldn't resist asking, "To do what?"

TWO

Unexpectedly, he dropped down to his haunches, bringing his eyes level with hers. Again she caught the tantalizing woodsy scent of cologne and couldn't help remembering how Brian had considered cologne somewhat unmanly. That was the last word in the world she'd use to describe Martin.

But it had always surprised her that a man who walked around looking like an unmade bed would bother wearing cologne, particularly such a distinctive, sophisticated fragrance. Somehow she sensed he might be capable of more surprises and felt a shiver of danger. If he was close enough for her to smell his cologne, then he was too close.

"Instead of collaborating, how about we turn this into a little contest?" The soft, measured words shimmered with challenge, like the blue eyes holding hers with such unflinching steadiness.

Julia frowned, deeply suspicious, but curiosity won out. "What kind of contest?"

"A contest to see who could write the better article."

Taken aback, she paused for a long moment before giving a cautious nod. "Continue."

"We each write the piece our own way, then submit them to Roger anonymously and get him to pick the better one."

"He'll hit the roof! After all, he told us to collaborate. Besides, I don't understand why you'd want to do this." Martin would do anything for a story, why would he propose something he might risk losing?

His faint smile had a cynical edge. "Let's just say I like to keep things interesting. And Roger only cares about the end product. He doesn't have to know anything about this until it's over. So what do you think? Are you game?"

Against all her warning instincts she felt a stirring of excitement. After two months of frustration she had a chance to prove herself, particularly to Martin, and demand the professional respect she wanted from him. Besides, it would be months before he was gone and she got this chance again.

"Maybe . . . I'll have to think about it."

Martin brushed an errant dark blond strand off his forehead with one hand. "What's the matter? Afraid?"

Was he psychic? It was almost as if he guessed how unsure she felt right now about pitting herself against him. His forceful presence filled the tiny office and threatened to engulf her.

"I'm not afraid. You act like this is some sort of game. It's not a game. It's my job. I don't take it lightly."

"Yeah . . . you're afraid." With a condescending smile, he stood up and shoved his hands into the pockets of his tan corduroy pants, squaring his broad shoulders as he looked down at her.

He had far too much raw masculinity for her taste. It made her feel overwhelmed and defensive. "Now, just a minute . . ."

"Look, Bennett," his voice hardened, "your hostility over the past two months hasn't escaped my notice."

"My hostility!" She would have jumped to her feet, but that would have brought her within inches of his face. She felt trapped in the chair. "Anyone would be hostile faced with your abundant arrogance."

He laughed. "My dear Bennett—I beg your pardon, *Julia* . . ." Hearing him wrap that husky English voice around her first name was profoundly unsettling. Only the familiar note of sarcasm saved her from complete disorientation. "That's the pot calling the kettle black, wouldn't you say? It's ironic really. I thought redheads were supposed to be so warm and passionate. But I've never met a more cold, arrogant, unapproachable woman—a veritable ice maiden."

Beneath the rush of sudden anger she felt an unexpected stab of pain. "How dare you presume to judge me!" She stood abruptly, sending the chair rolling backwards, not caring anymore how close he was. "You don't even know me. I'm sick and tired of you making me feel like I'm the one with the problem. If I had my choice, I'd rather be an ice maiden than an unscrupulous carpetbagger!"

Complete silence reigned in the tiny cubicle as Julia stared at him, appalled, and saw only impassivity on his face. Her heart raced wildly against her ribs. In spite of her best intentions, how did they get into this name calling?

Taking a step backward, she struggled to calm her rapid breathing. "Look, this is getting us nowhere. We have to work together." Fighting down the mortification and hurt, she could barely keep her voice from trembling. "I suggest we both calm down and forget this unfortunate conversation ever happened." But inside she still felt sick at the openness with which they'd expressed their dislike.

He had wanted to provoke her, but now he felt

ashamed of himself. But something about this woman got under his skin. "For once I think you're right, Bennett."

He walked slowly around the desk and took his chair again as she sank down into hers. He could see a faint flush on her cheekbones.

"So what do you say?" He tried to bring things back to business. "Are you interested in my proposal?" Raising his eyebrows a fraction, Martin tipped his head a little to one side. "It'll give you a chance to get even."

The words brought a faint smile to her lips that surprised him. As smiles went, it didn't light up the room, but at least it was an improvement on the way she usually looked right through him.

After hesitating a moment, she nodded. "You've got a deal." Taking a deep breath, Julia could feel the heat receding from her cheeks. "Now what are the rules?"

He looked both satisfied and amused by her response. "There are none. Just remember, darling, all's fair in love and war."

"As long as you remember that I'm not your darling." Julia returned his smile with a sudden tremor of reckless excitement. She must be lightheaded from the anticipation of this unorthodox test.

"How very true." His narrowed eyes were thoughtful and appraising. "How very true."

She felt a tingle of apprehension. She'd better be on her mettle from this moment on. She had no doubt his instincts, sharpened by years spent living on the edge of danger, were as finely honed as the rebel fighters he'd spent months trailing through the jungles of Colombia. No, he wouldn't make it easy for her. Rising to her feet, she held out her hand.

He stared at it for a moment, then reached across the desk. Her hand felt warm and small in his own, so slender and fragile it seemed he could crush her bones with very little effort, yet her grip was firm and strong.

Julia withdrew her hand, feeling awkward. He had held it a little too long, as if he didn't plan on letting it go. She wished she could figure this man out.

"I've got a hot lead to follow, so I'll be on my way." With a tight smile, she spun on her heel.

"See you on the battleground, Bennett," he called after her. As she walked away, he couldn't help but notice the sway of her slender hips in the narrow navy skirt. What would she look like in jeans? He grinned. This contest could turn out to be very entertaining.

On the way back to her own tiny cubicle, Julia paused at Eunice's desk. "Would you be a doll and book me a room at the George in Niagara-on-the-Lake for tomorrow night?"

"Sure, no problem. So what's happening?" The secretary's good-humored face betrayed her eager interest. "Who's doing the story?"

"We both are."

Eunice clearly knew all about the argument and was just dying for more information, but Julia couldn't satisfy her curiosity without news of their contest going all around the office and coming right back to Roger within minutes. Besides, she had an appointment to keep.

A few minutes later, on her way toward the elevators, she saw Martin leaning on the secretary's desk in earnest conversation. What was he digging out of her? Judging by the speed of Eunice's mouth, a lot.

Julia sat tapping her fingernails on the steering wheel and glanced up uneasily at the NO STOPPING sign. Hadn't he said he'd be ready and waiting for her at eleven? It was now five past and still no sign of him on the Front Street sidewalk in front of his building.

With an impatient sigh she got out of her car. Thank

goodness there was no snow on the ground yet in this unseasonably mild winter. But the February morning air still felt bitterly cold as she hurried up the brick walkway toward the upscale glass and brick condominium tower and into the warmth of the main lobby.

After pressing the buzzer three times, she finally got a response.

"Yes? Who is it?"

Who did he think it was, the Avon lady? "It's Julia."

"Oh, is it that time already? I have to finish packing. Why don't you come up?"

Go up to his apartment and wait for him? That sounded a little too cozy. "I'm in a tow-away zone. I'd better stay with the car."

"Suit yourself." She could almost see his nonchalant shrug. "I'll only be a minute."

Fifteen minutes later she watched Martin emerge from the building carrying a large blue nylon sports bag in one hand and the ubiquitous knapsack slung over his other shoulder.

He opened the door and gave her an unconcerned smile as he tossed his bags into the back, then swung into the passenger seat. He looked set for the Arctic in a rugged navy parka that accentuated the breadth of his shoulders and deepened the blue of his eyes.

"So what are we waiting for?"

Julia stared at him in amazement. That was it? No apology for keeping her waiting? The man was impossible. She put the car in gear and waited for the opportunity to merge with the busy downtown traffic.

"I know where you were yesterday afternoon." He made it sound as if she'd been up to something scandalous. "I have to admit I didn't expect you to be so quick off the mark."

"What are you talking about?"

"I'm talking about Dr. McLaughlin."

"Oh . . . you saw her too, did you?"

Well, after all, it only made sense that, like her, he would head straight for the Royal Ontario Museum to talk to the archaeologist in charge of the excavation.

The small, voluble scientist had taken her down into the basement labs and shown her the bones discovered by Niagara Parks Commission workers digging the foundation for a picnic shelter. The doctor had concluded that the men had fallen in heavy bush and never been buried. She had also determined, from the buttons on their jackets, that the bodies were those of two high-ranking American officers, two British officers, and a civilian. The excavation had also uncovered over two hundred Spanish silver coins.

Concentrating on getting around the flotillas of trucks on the expressway, Julia stole a quick glance at the lake on her left. It lay cold and gray under a flat, dull sky. Niagara was almost directly due south on the other side.

So Martin had talked to Dr. McLaughlin. But did he know that the excavation site was a couple of miles upriver from Fort George, where the main battle of the American invasion and subsequent occupation took place? The fort was a mile from the town of Niagara-on-the-Lake, which in those days was known as Newark and had been occupied by the American troops from May to December of 1813. Julia smiled to herself. Maybe not. That snippet of information had come from her secret sources.

After leaving the museum she'd immediately phoned the major in Ottawa, where he was working with the Defense Department. In his usual prompt fashion, her father had referred her to an expert military historian at the War Museum who specialized in the War of 1812 and was only too happy to help Major Bennett's daughter.

The moment retired Colonel Hathi heard her name

and the reason for her call he'd erupted in an enthusiastic monologue of information.

"I saw that news report and I thought there was something damned fishy about the whole thing, don't you think?" he interrogated in a parade-ground voice.

Julia agreed, carefully holding the phone away from her ear while the colonel continued his rambling tirade about what business high-ranking officers had skirmishing in the bush.

"And where the hell were their men, may I ask? Answer me that!"

Naturally she couldn't and said good-bye to the colonel shortly after. Dad put her on to a real live one there, but she had gleaned some useful information.

"You look like the cat that swallowed the cream," Martin said as the skyline of downtown Toronto receded in the rearview mirror.

Julia's smile broadened. "It's just that I'm getting really excited about this story. I'm discovering how much I don't know about that war and it's fascinating."

"You actually look like you're enjoying this."

She looked over and saw him regarding her with surprise. What did he expect? That she'd be shaking in her boots at the prospect of being in competition with him?

"Yes, I am. You know, my father always said competitiveness brought out the best in people and I'm beginning to see he's right. So I just want you to know that I have every intention of beating the pants off you."

Martin smiled to himself. "Well now, there's an intriguing prospect."

He saw her dart him a quick glance and his smile broadened. To his surprise he noticed a flush spreading along her cheekbones and she fixed her eyes on the expressway again. Her reaction to the innuendo amazed him. He'd fully expected one of her scornful looks.

The kind that told him she considered him little better than a vulgar savage.

Driving through the dreary urban sprawl curving around the lake from Toronto, they were silent for quite some time. Martin unzipped his parka and settled his long, lean body more comfortably in the bucket seat. She felt supremely conscious of him so close beside her, making the compact Escort feel even smaller.

"Maps in here I presume?" he asked, already leaning over to open the glove compartment and pulling out her road map of southern Ontario. Something dropped out of the folds of the map and he bent to pick it up.

"Isn't this the chap who used to meet you after work?"

Julia glanced over and stiffened with dismay when she saw the snapshot in Martin's hand. A picture of her and Brian at his sister's wedding. The day Brian had dropped his little bombshell.

"Poor sod, what did he do to earn that look from you?"

Nothing much, except tell her that he had the rest of her life planned out and that her wishes had nothing to do with it. She had been too upset and indignant to notice the Polaroid being snapped until the photographer had handed her the picture.

"Please do me a favor and put that away."

"Ah . . . still nursing a broken heart?"

She almost thought she heard a little compassion behind the question. Julia shrugged. "I'll survive."

The last person she wanted to discuss it with was Martin Taylor, who thought her such *a veritable ice maiden*. She squirmed in her seat. Why did his opinion bother her so much?

"Well, here's a friendly word of advice. We men aren't worth all the anguish women expend on us."

Julia looked over and caught a cynical little smile tilting one corner of his mouth.

She was beginning to think he was right. The breakup had hurt, but what had hurt more was the realization that Brian Harrington not only didn't really love her but barely knew her. He just saw her as the perfect senior partner's wife. Someone cool, poised, and immaculately turned out to grace his arm at the Law Society dinner.

He'd scarcely given a thought to the idea she might have needs of her own that went beyond dedicating her life to furthering his career. The discovery that Brian could never once put anybody before himself had left her deeply hurt and disappointed. And she had thought she loved him. The memory still rankled.

"Please don't think I'm pining away, waiting for a man to come along and make my life worthwhile. I'm not. I like my independence. I love my job. I own my own home. I'm very happy with my life, thank you."

Julia clamped her mouth shut, stunned by her own vehemence. But she'd had to go through this once too often with her father. He still couldn't understand why she and Brian had broken up.

"Tell me," Martin asked with dry gravity. "Are we a complete waste of space? Do men not have any useful function in your scheme of things?"

"Hmm . . . maybe to take out the garbage."

She couldn't repress a grin, and Martin gave a shout of laughter that was so genuine and infectious it surprised her. Perhaps working with him wouldn't be so difficult after all. Still, she was relieved to see him toss the photo back in the glove compartment and open up the map.

Her father had always encouraged her to be strong and self-reliant, but he still thought every woman needed a man to make her complete. Julia gave a wistful smile. His little girl was twenty-seven now and knew she needed more than that. She needed a home. And for all its shortcomings, she'd take her own tiny house over the cold perfection of Brian's mansion any day.

Six months ago she had stood in the kitchen of the cramped, run-down two-story in the east end of Toronto, looked out onto the steep clay bluffs and the perfect blue curve of the lake dotted with white sails, and promptly fallen in love. It had taken every penny of her savings and a frightening chunk of her monthly pay, but it was hers. Home. In a way that no house had ever been before. Not like the temporary quarters, the rented apartments in which she'd spent her childhood.

She loved to spend every spare hour stripping wallpaper and refinishing woodwork. All the hard work required to make the house livable just made her feel more rooted, satisfied a soul-deep craving for connection.

Her mother might have chosen to follow her father around the world from one posting to another, paying the price of constant instability, but that was one hardship Julia knew she would never impose on her own children. Every place had been just temporary. Schools, friends, all temporary. How she had hated that rootlessness. Now she had a home at last—one she had made for herself.

They had left the expressway far behind, finally reaching the orchards and vineyards of Niagara. Spread out over the flat landscape on either side of the road, serried rows of small bare trees lay exposed to the chill gray sky.

Driving down the last mile of long, straight road toward the town, it hit Julia that there was no turning back. During the ride down they had established a rapport that had surprised her. But now, as the clapboard saltboxes and gabled brick houses flashed by, she realized—the contest was on.

"I'm sorry, but I won't have time to drop you at your hotel," she told Martin.

As it was, she was already late for her one o'clock

appointment with the head curator at the historic fort just on the other side of town. Turning onto Queen Street, she drove down the broad, quiet thoroughfare lined with quaint nineteenth-century storefronts.

"That's all right. You can let me off here." He indicated the red brick clock tower set in the middle of the street, just before the main crossroads.

She pulled over and Martin climbed out, retrieving his bags from the backseat, before ducking his head back into the car. "Thanks for the lift."

"I don't expect I'll be seeing much of you, but good luck." She held out her hand toward him.

"Well that's damned sporting of you, old girl." He shook her hand and smiled, a devilish light in his blue eyes.

He was a man who always looked as if he was up to something, as if he had an ace up his sleeve. She'd do well to remember that. He might have been unexpectedly amicable on the ride down, but he was a formidable opponent and the contest had only just begun.

Swinging his bags up onto his shoulder, Martin strode off down the street. Not like the stranger he was, but with the confident air of a man intimately acquainted with his surroundings.

With a slight shake of her head, Julia put the car in gear and headed for the fort.

"Come in, come in out of that damp cold. Come in, child, and get warm. You must be Julia Bennett."

Julia paused in her struggle to close the heavy wooden door of the George Inn. She looked across the dim lobby at the small gray-haired woman emerging from a doorway under the carved oak staircase. With a smile creasing her lined face, the woman bustled over, shut the door, and relieved Julia of the overnight bag, leaving her with only her suitcase and bulging briefcase to deal with.

". . . and how was your drive down from Toronto?" she continued in a breathless voice, plopping Julia's heavy duffel bag down on the well-worn red carpet. Going behind the desk set in an alcove beside the stairs, she opened the large registration book.

"It's so nice to have visitors. We don't get too many here in the winter. But, you know, I think you picked the best time of year to see our little town. It gets much too overcrowded during the theater festival . . ."

Julia put down her suitcase and flexed her cramped, cold fingers, then reached for the pen the proprietress held out to her as the woman continued.

"I'm Amy Balfour. My husband Jim and I run the inn, but he's away on business right now and I'm holding the fort by myself."

"I'm pleased to meet you, Mrs. Balfour."

"Just call me Amy. We don't stand on ceremony much around here. And I'll call you Julia, or do you prefer Julie?"

"Julia, please . . ." She smiled back at Amy's unaffected friendliness. "I can't tell you how happy I am to be here. Every time I've come down to Niagara-on-the-Lake for the day I've noticed your inn and promised myself that if I ever stayed here, I'd stay at the George. It sounds silly, but it almost called to me."

Her gaze swept around the small entrance hall, the old-fashioned wallpaper embossed with roses and bluebirds. The interior was every bit as charming as the blue colonial clapboard facade.

Through an open doorway on her right, she glimpsed the flickering orange light of a log fire in the hearth. Just the sight of that cheerful blaze in this oasis of peace and quiet made her feel warm.

"Well, isn't that nice, dear," Amy beamed at her. "We're not as big as some, but we pride ourselves on making people feel at home."

Julia nodded. Ever since she stepped across the

threshold she'd felt as if she were being enfolded in the arms of a loving family. It was hard not to respond to the landlady's gentle warmth as she reminisced about the Balfours' long association with the eighteenth-century inn.

Nodding in bemusement at Amy's nonstop chatter, Julia looked down to sign the register and the smile froze on her lips.

". . . It never rains but it pours." The innkeeper's soft voice washed over Julia as she stared at that bold signature. "We only have one other guest and he's from Toronto, too."

With a dazed sense of doom, Julia read the black scrawl that naturally had to take up two lines in the leather-bound register.

With five other hotels in this tourist town, how was it possible he had picked the same one? Then, with the image clearly etched in her memory, she saw him perched on Eunice's desk. Of course. She turned her eyes heavenward. *Thank you, Eunice.*

Almost on cue, she heard a jaunty footfall descending the stairs and a familiar whistle. Through the oak railing, a pair of corduroy-clad legs appeared. He stopped a couple of steps short of the hall and the whistle died away as he stared down at her, his eyes widening in astonishment.

Boy, he was good. That surprise almost looked genuine.

"Blimey . . . if this isn't a coincidence. Imagine both of us picking the same hotel."

"Yes, imagine that." As if he could fool her with that choirboy innocence. Now she knew the reason for that unholy amusement she'd seen kindling in his eyes when she said they wouldn't be seeing much of each other. He'd been laughing at her all along.

His eyes narrowed as he came down the last few

steps and stood before her in the hall. She could see he'd sensed her displeasure.

"Oh, do you two know each other?" Amy cut in, her expectant gaze going from one to the other.

"You could say that," Julia replied dryly.

"And you're right next door to each other, too," the landlady exclaimed, spreading her hands in delight.

"I must have died and gone to hell," Julia muttered under her breath as she stooped to pick up her briefcase.

Martin felt a grin spread over his face. Was this the same woman he'd written off as too restrained to be human?

"Pardon, dear?" Amy's good-humored smile held a hint of uncertainty.

"She said . . . she knows me well," Martin filled in, paying no attention to Julia's astonished gasp as he took the briefcase from her hand and tucked her unresisting fingers into the crook of his arm.

Ignoring her glare, he shot her a guileless smile. "Julia, darling, let's take a walk." He could feel her trying to pull away and he patted her hand, holding it even tighter and began leading her toward the front door. Before she jumped to all the wrong conclusions, he'd better explain.

"Not right now, Martin. Perhaps later." She smiled through tightly clenched teeth and with surprising reluctance he allowed her to wrench her hand away from his arm.

Julia turned back toward Amy. "It's been a long drive and I just want to go to my room."

She needed to get away from him. And not a minute too soon. The disturbing sensation that had taken her by surprise still lingered on her fingertips, even though she wasn't touching him anymore. Beneath the slippery parka, beneath the springiness of his wool sweater, she had felt the hard, unyielding curve of his bicep under her hand, her fingers molding around him with unexpected intimacy. Shouldering her duffel bag, she reached for her cases, rebuffing his attempt to help.

"We really should have a little *chat,* don't you think?" He shoved his hands in his pockets, watching her as she straightened up, his meaningful look not lost on her.

"Perhaps later," she replied with a cool edge to her voice. Her eyes slid over him dismissively before turning to Amy with a warm smile. "I'd like to see my room now, if you don't mind."

"Of course, dear." The landlady was all bustle as she led her up the stairs. "And how about a nice cup of tea? I can bring it to you, or you can come down to the lounge if you prefer . . ."

Julia followed the chattering little figure, but a quick glance at Martin standing in the lobby watching her left her uneasy. The ominous gleam in his narrowed eyes told her she wouldn't be able to avoid him for long. She hurried after Amy, disappearing around the top of the staircase, as Martin began whistling again and she suddenly recognized the tune. *The 1812 Overture.* She stumbled on the last step with her heavy suitcase and cursed under her breath. Her winter coat was suddenly much too warm and she felt unspeakably flustered.

"Now the bathroom's right here beside you at the end of the hall, and . . . here we are." Amy threw open the door and Julia found herself in a small square corner room. "I've left the window open a crack to air out the room because it hasn't been used since the summer. Close it if you get too chilly."

There was no danger of that. She felt positively suffocated with heat. Julia pulled off her heavy wool coat, throwing it on the blue nine-patch quilt covering the carved ebony bed.

Promising to put the kettle on, Amy left and Julia stepped over to the long window, parting the lace curtains to gaze out at the view. Beyond the white wooden railings of the upstairs veranda she could see bare trees and the mouth of the Niagara River, where it met the lake, reflecting the full pewter of the late afternoon sky. She allowed the lace curtains to fall back into place and turned to the darkening room with a sigh.

What was she going to do about Martin Taylor? What could she do? She didn't have the right to kick him out and she had no intention of leaving. After finally getting the opportunity to stay in this charming little inn, she wasn't about to be driven away. With a decisive nod she heaved her suitcase onto the bed and unzipped it.

He'd warned her there were no rules and now it looked as though he was throwing the first curve. *All right, Mr. Taylor, I'm ready for you.*

But first things first. Get out of her suit and into something more comfortable. She threw the case open and pulled out the contents, rummaging for her dark green sweats.

Suddenly there was a knock at her door and the sound of Martin's voice. "Bennett, are you in there? We need to talk."

Instinctively she moved toward the door as her heart began to beat rapidly. "What's there to talk about?"

"Plenty. But we can't talk like this. Come on, open up. Let me in."

She clutched her hands tightly in front of her. "I don't think so. I know what you're up to and it's not going to work."

"I'm not up to anything. For God's sakes, this is ridiculous. Come on, open up . . . Oh." He paused for a second. "Hi, Amy."

After a moment she heard a door shut and a soft knock on her own door. She opened it to find Amy with an armload of towels and a curious look on her face. Julia murmured her thanks as she took the towels and chuckled as she shut her door, dropped them on the dresser, and went back to her suitcase.

After stripping off the tailored navy skirt and jacket and crisp white blouse, Julia sat down on the bed and peeled off her pantyhose with a blissful sigh. The cool air felt wonderfully refreshing on her overheated skin as she stepped over to the large old-fashioned wardrobe by the bed and began hanging up her clothes.

Obviously Martin hoped that if he bugged her enough she'd give up and go tearing back to Toronto. But he had a lot to learn about her, the first thing being that she could handle just about anything he threw at her.

The scraping noise behind her made her whirl around, dumbfounded with shock to see a brown hiking boot, then a leg encased in tan corduroy coming through her window. A moment later they were followed by a blond head and Martin Taylor's bearded face framed incongruously by the antique lace curtains.

He froze half in, half out the window while his stricken eyes slowly traveled the length of her barely clad body.

THREE

"What are you doing here?" Julia gasped.

He supposed a gentleman would jump back out again, but Martin just paused and stared. Continuing to straddle the windowsill, he found himself unable to tear his gaze away from her slender, elegantly manicured hands. More precisely, from their desperate, unsuccessful efforts to conceal her breasts, barely covered by the flimsy peach lace bra. He saw her frantic eyes dart to the open suitcase and the mound of clothes on her bed.

"Get out!" she screeched, making a dive for a white terry robe and holding it up in front of her like a shield.

"Calm down. I just want to talk . . ." Shaking off the bemusement that had kept him frozen in the window, Martin eased himself fully through the frame and into the room. "And lower your voice. Do you want everyone in the house to hear you?"

"How dare you come creeping in like this . . . without even knocking!"

Her tone had dropped to a whispered hiss, and he had to suppress a smirk at her automatic compliance.

"I did knock."

That flustered her for a moment, he could see it in

her face. "I don't care. You have no right to be here." Her voice rose again as she fumbled with her robe in a panic-stricken attempt to cover herself.

He forced his eyes away from her toward the window. "Look, Julia, we need to talk before we go any further. And if you won't let me in, I'll find a way to get to you. I'm not going to let you shut me out."

"You and I have nothing to talk about." Her voice was trembling and breathless with agitation.

He darted a quick glance and saw that the armholes in her robe were eluding her. He turned his gaze to the window again, but nothing could erase the memory of her long, slender legs and the feminine curve of her hips, scarcely clad in another alluring scrap of silk, and her small, high, rounded breasts.

But once again he couldn't resist the temptation and turned his head toward her. He noticed her shudder as she wrestled with the robe. A stiff, cold breeze was coming in the window and she obviously needed warming up. The urge to wrap his arms around her and do the job himself took him by surprise.

Something about the combination of her barely clad body and her delicate floral scent was assaulting his senses in the most disturbing way. Before he got himself into even deeper trouble, he'd better help her out. He went over and, keeping his eyes strictly on the job at hand, untangled the sleeves of the robe and held it out for her to put on.

"Believe me, I deplore my method, but you weren't cooperating, and we do need to talk." He looked away and smothered an inward sigh. This was a hell of a time for his conscience to barge in.

A quick glance told her that Martin's gaze was studiously trained on the view outside the window, his face expressionless.

"Not cooperate with you?" She gave the semblance

of a laugh, more nervous than sarcastic. "Whatever gave you that idea?"

She slipped her arms in, jerking away from the momentary contact of his fingers on her bare shoulders. He stood between her and the door, and with the bed on one side and the wall behind her, she felt cornered and ridiculously panicky. She needed to get as far away from him as possible.

Unwilling to brush past him in case he tried to stop her, she made her escape by scrambling crablike over the bed to stand on the other side.

"Well . . . why are you still standing there? What are you grinning at?" And why couldn't she stop blabbering on like a dimwit? Let *him* defend himself. Let him justify crawling in through her window like a second-rate cat burglar.

Julia clamped her lips shut and wrapped the robe tightly around her shivering body, trying to clutch back the shreds of her dignity after such an inelegant flight.

But he said nothing, just stood watching her, his eyes brimming with laughter. Now she felt more determined than ever to beat him at his own game. If this was another attempt to make things tough for her, then he had a lot to learn about Julia Bennett. What was it the major used to say when she quailed at the prospect of yet another new school, another set of strange faces? *Never let them rattle you. Stay in control.* She lifted her chin and summoned every ounce of composure.

"You're right, we do need to talk," she said, forgetting her resolve of a few moments before to maintain a dignified silence. "When are you moving?"

He held her gaze for a second, then walked over toward the window. For an instant she thought he was about to exit the same outrageous way he'd come in, but he simply shut the open window, then turned back to her.

"I was here first. If anyone should leave . . ."

"Oh no, you don't. We both know you deliberately chose this hotel because you knew I was booked in and you wanted to bug me. Well, you have."

Let him think he'd achieved his objective. She had to stay one step ahead of him and not show her hand or she'd be lost.

Incredulity flickered across Martin's face as he watched her through the gathering gloom. Slowly she became aware of the thick silence of the old inn, the absence of traffic noise in the quiet street outside as she waited silently for his next move.

"You don't seriously believe I'd do something so childish on purpose, do you?"

Julia laughed. "Come on, why don't you drop the game?" She noticed his eyes widening in surprise. "It was a good try, but it didn't work. It'll take a lot more than you staying at the same hotel to make me turn tail and run home."

He settled his narrow hips on the windowsill and stroked a hand over his bearded chin in bemusement. "You astonish me."

With his long legs stretched out in front of him, he crossed his arms, leaning back against the pane, for all the world as if talking to her half dressed in her bedroom was an everyday occurrence.

"You just don't know me very well. You thought I'd be a pushover. Well, think again."

Julia couldn't help feeling intensely amused at the disorienting effect her behavior was obviously having on him. Served him right for pegging her as a cold, stuck-up prig. But she shouldn't be so complacent. She'd been just as guilty of making snap judgments about him.

He brushed back the sun-streaked blond strands that flopped persistently over his forehead, a thoughtful frown between his brows as he regarded her steadily.

"Look, this is silly. I came up here to suggest we call a truce."

"You don't expect me to be so gullible, do you?"

He gave her a blank stare.

"You did a good job lulling me into a false sense of security on the way down, but you're not going to do it again. You made it very clear yesterday that the gloves were off. I don't know about you, but I'm beginning to enjoy this little power play. I don't think I want to dilute it with a truce."

She tilted her chin a little, as cool and businesslike as if they were facing each other across a boardroom table, not a clothing-strewn bed. He took a moment to weigh her words with a puzzled astonishment she found intensely gratifying.

"You have to admit we do have a problem. It'll be impossible to avoid each other—the town's too small. Don't you agree that we've got to come to some sort of an arrangement?"

"Yes, I do agree." Julia bit her lip, trying to suppress a grin to no avail. "I suppose we could always ignore each other." She couldn't hide her amusement at seeing their usual roles turned on their heads. Martin Taylor, of all people, being conciliatory and reasonable.

Dawning recognition sparked in his blue eyes. "You're laughing at me, Julia Bennett, and you're enjoying it, aren't you?"

And then she did laugh out loud. "I'm sorry. It was too good an opportunity to miss."

He laughed, too, but the amusement in his eyes held an ironic glint as he sobered. His glance slid away from her and she was surprised to see he almost looked uncomfortable. He cleared his throat and looked at her again. "You know, Julia, perhaps this contest business isn't such a good idea after all."

She waited, tensing a little. Was he going to suggest she pack it in and go home? Use this inexplicable moment of camaraderie to his advantage? Maybe he figured that taking the reasonable approach would achieve more than his bullying did before.

"We should work on this together."

"You mean collaborate?" It couldn't have shocked her more if he'd suggested they fly to the moon together.

He gave a casual shrug, but she sensed something uncertain in him that confused her. This wasn't like him.

"That's what Roger told us to do."

She shook her head, feeling a little dazed. "Yes, but you said . . ."

"I said a lot of stupid things. Let's forget them and start all over, shall we?"

"No!"

Her vehement denial took him aback. "I beg your pardon?"

"I mean, no, I don't want to collaborate," she said, surprising herself, and him, judging by his raised eyebrows.

And she didn't want to collaborate with him. Not only because she wanted to do this on her own, but also because, after that disturbing little episode downstairs, she didn't want to spend any more time with him than she had to.

"Look, Julia . . ."

"No, Martin. Let's just stick to our original plan. And as far as us both being here, just because we're confined to the same town doesn't mean we have to live in each other's back pockets."

"Oh, I see. You go your way and I go mine." He shrugged and smiled, but there was something about the smile she didn't quite trust. "Well, I suppose it's better than open warfare. But how about when we're not working? Do we still go our separate ways?"

"Of course. Just because we're guests at the same hotel . . ."

"I know, I know. We don't have to live in each other's back pockets. Okay." He nodded, apparently accepting her terms.

Part of her felt relieved. Putting their silly antagonism aside would free her to concentrate her energies on the job ahead. But she also felt wary. She'd need all her wits about her to cope with Martin. She must never underestimate him again. When it came to the wiliness and canny instincts that made him a top-notch journalist, he was the master and she was a mere babe in the woods. She'd be a fool to forget that.

She walked decisively around the end of the bed and approached him. "So . . . we call a truce."

He rose swiftly to his feet and stepped closer. Julia looked up at him, suddenly aware again of her bare feet and short terry robe, and felt a quiver of tension. She couldn't get too smug just because she'd momentarily thrown him off.

"Oh, and by the way, one further thing that I want to make clear. My chauffeuring services ended when we got here. I may be a sporting old girl, but I'm not *that* sporting."

He grinned. "Never fear, fair lady, yonder lies my trusty steed." He waved toward the window.

Parked across the street, Julia spied the oldest, most decrepit vehicle she had ever seen. In some previous lifetime it had been a Honda, possibly brown, although it was hard to tell with the blue replacement door and patches of red primer where the body had been repaired.

Julia shook her head. "If I were you, I'd be careful I didn't get pulled over and fined . . . for littering."

He grinned again and extended his hand. She slowly held out her own, returning the pressure of his warm, firm grip with an assertive handshake designed to tell him he wouldn't find her a sitting target.

"Shall we go to our corners?" That wicked gleam was in his eyes again.

This might be a truce, but the war was most definitely still on.

The firelight flickered on the beamed ceiling and caught in miniature reflections on the lenses of Martin's tortoiseshell-framed glasses. His long, lean frame lay sprawled along the length of the old chintz sofa, bearded chin propped on the fist of one muscular arm left bare by the rolled up shirt sleeve. He chewed the end of his pencil and gazed into the flames.

From the depths of the old armchair by the fire Julia watched his abstraction with a curious eye. Against her will, she found herself becoming fascinated by him, as she would be fascinated by a sleek jungle cat lying deceptively quiescent, knowing at any moment it could pounce and tear her to shreds. The comparison left her unsettled and strengthened her determination to keep him at arm's length. Yet she couldn't help but watch him.

It must be the reading glasses. They gave his face a studious, reflective quality totally foreign to the pretentious braggart she knew. He sat lost in whatever thoughts filled his head as he listened to Amy telling them about the history of the town and jotted down the occasional note on the pad at his elbow.

"There've been Balfours living right here for over two hundred years." Amy pulled at the ball of wool and resumed her knitting, a voluminous blue afghan that covered her lap and almost touched the floor.

Julia watched her placid movements as she rocked back and forth. The large bentwood took up the corner on the other side of the stone hearth, where the black iron fire implements hung. Every now and then Amy would lean forward, take the poker, and prod the glowing birch log, sending a shower of sparks up the chimney.

"Jebediah Balfour built the first inn on this spot in 1790, when Niagara was the capital of Upper Canada. They called it Newark then. It was a thriving center of trade."

Julia wrapped her arms around her knees and pulled them closer to her chest. She still couldn't believe she was sitting here in this intimate setting, her eyes repeatedly drawn to the man who, twenty-four hours before, she would have done anything to avoid.

"Of course, this isn't the original building." Amy's fingers moved steadily and the needles flashed in the firelight. "The Americans burned the town in December of 1813, when they were forced to end their eight-month occupation and retreat back across the river. Very little was left standing and the inn wasn't spared. It was rebuilt around this very chimney on top of the original foundations, but enlarged and improved. We Balfours are a tenacious bunch."

No kidding. Refusing Amy's kindly offer of cocoa in the lounge would have required a rudeness Julia simply couldn't contemplate. After spending the rest of the day wandering around the town, she had eaten a greasy burger at the diner, just to avoid facing Martin.

In spite of their truce, the last thing she wanted, or expected, was to find herself in this impossibly cozy, almost romantic, setting. But she hadn't missed the shrewd assessing look he had shot her, telling her he knew very well why she had made herself scarce that afternoon.

"After they built Fort George, the inn was a popular place for the officers. In fact there's a very interesting story concerning a wounded young captain who took refuge in this inn and eventually died here."

Julia shivered as an icy chill ran down her spine. She

snuggled into the comforting warmth of the overstuffed armchair and glanced at Martin. He was still toying with the pencil, running the eraser thoughtfully over his mouth. Without meaning to, her eyes traced the movement of the pencil against the line of his lips. They were firm and well shaped, unobscured by the short beard, and she knew that when he smiled they revealed strong, even white teeth. Some women in the office found his smile quite devastating.

Almost hypnotically fascinated by his mouth, she suddenly realized the pencil had slowed, then stopped. She lifted her gaze to his eyes and found him watching her with a thoughtful, hooded expression. Did he even see her, or was his mind far away in the sad story Amy was telling?

". . . so they took him in and hid him in the cellar while American officers sat in the taproom above, drinking a toast to their occupation of the town. But the fever set in, and though the daughter of the house nursed him night and day for two weeks, poor Young Captain Fairfax eventually succumbed to his wounds. They couldn't risk taking him out, so they buried him in the cellar and he lies there still."

Swallowing a lump in her throat, Julia stared into the shimmering flames through the tears filling her eyes.

". . . and the saddest part of all," Amy's pale blue eyes misted over, "was his last wish. To get home to his wife and their first child. The baby he never, ever saw."

In a sudden wave of pity and anguish, Julia felt the pain of the young widow's grief, the loneliness of the child who never knew its father. She choked back a muffled sob and stared into the fire, afraid to turn her head and see Martin's mocking gaze on her.

"And Sarah Balfour, who nursed him, kept his diary. I've read it myself and I feel as if I knew that young man." Amy's square, capable hands had stilled, her knitting needles poised in mid-stitch as she stared off into the darkened outer reaches of the room, where the firelight threw huge shadows on the far wall. "It made me think of all the boys garrisoned here during the last war. Jim and I were courting then . . . he went overseas, too." Her voice softened to a sigh. "Some of them didn't make it back."

"Why wasn't the diary ever returned to his wife?"

The echo of sadness in Martin's quiet voice gave Julia an uncomfortable jolt. So it hadn't left him untouched either. How could a man, apparently so jaded by the horrors he had reported, be affected by an old sentimental story like this?

"Because his young nurse had fallen in love with him. You see, it wasn't found until Jim's great-grandfather's day when they were enlarging the root cellar and came across a battered old tin box. Inside were the diary and a few pitiful treasures that had belonged to Sarah Balfour, including her own journal."

"Whatever happened to her?" Martin asked. Julia leaned forward to catch Amy's next words.

"Ah . . . well, now the records say she died of influenza a few months later. I find it hard to believe a young, healthy girl of seventeen would succumb to influenza. I think . . ." Her voice dropped to a low, confiding murmur and trembled slightly. "*I* think that she died of a broken heart." Her knitting forgotten, she rested her hands on the soft folds of blue wool as she stared into the flames.

Complete silence filled the room and a log popped in the fireplace. Julia gazed into the flames, watching them lick blue and orange around the charred wood. Then Martin straightened up on the sofa and swung his feet to the floor. The soft thud of his Nikes hitting the carpet sounded unnaturally loud in the quiet room.

He stretched, arching his back and flexing the muscles in his shoulders as if to ease the stiffness in his body. Julia found herself noticing the tan oxford cloth tightening across his chest, the small brown buttons straining against the buttonholes.

"Thank you for telling us the story. I'd be very interested in seeing this diary." He began to rise.

"But the story isn't finished yet," Amy said quietly, and Martin took his seat again. Leaning forward, he rested his elbows on his knees, hands loosely knit between them.

"You see," her bright eyes slid from Martin to Julia, "our captain is not at rest."

One by one, every hair on the nape of Julia's neck prickled to attention. She struggled with the overpowering urge to look over her shoulder.

Martin chuckled. "You're not trying to tell me he's haunting the inn."

Amy's lips compressed in disapproval and she shot him a piercing look from beneath her brows. "Don't be so quick to laugh, young man. There's many a guest has met our captain."

He smiled indulgently. "I'll believe you, but I think you're scaring Julia."

"Don't be ridiculous." Julia bridled at his patronizing tone. "There's no such thing as ghosts. It was a wonderful story though and I think I'll use it." She smiled at Amy.

He laughed. "I'm glad you're so brave. Can I crawl in with you then, if something goes boo in the night?"

Julia caught Amy's interested gaze flicking back and forth between them. Then the older woman interjected with a smile, "Oh, no, Martin. Our Captain Fairfax is very discriminating. He only appears to the ladies."

Julia saw the amusement sparkling in his blue eyes as they sought hers across the fire-lit room. "Well, in that case, you can crawl in with me."

"Thanks, but I'll take my chances with the ghost," she responded dryly, but without warning an unwanted image invaded her mind of lying beside him on that soft feather bed above them, naked limbs entwined. Now where had that come from?

Julia struggled up from the cozy embrace of the old armchair and began saying her good nights. Suddenly the fire was too hot on her cheeks and the room felt unbearably stuffy.

She woke with a gasp, her body tingling, her heart pounding. Leaning on one elbow she groped for the bedside lamp and switched it on, pushing the hair out of her eyes to peer groggily at her wristwatch and find it was three A.M.

Julia flopped back on her pillow and stared at the faded green brocade canopy above her head, the dream replaying itself in disturbing detail . . . Captain Fairfax in his red coat and flashing gold epaulets, his boyish face split in an attractive grin. Looking up at a pretty young girl filling his tankard of ale, he had laughed joyfully and pulled her down into his lap.

Then suddenly she was the one in the young captain's arms and he was kissing her, his lips coaxing and clinging, his tongue entwining with hers, his fingers at the lacing of her bodice. Lost in a realm of pure sensation, she had surrendered to the intoxicating seduction of his mouth on hers, the erotic havoc his hands were creating on her sensitized breasts. And then he slowly drew back and she gazed, breathless and quivering, into passion-clouded eyes, as blue as the lake under summer skies. The eyes of Martin Taylor.

She threw back the covers and jumped out of bed, shivering in her long flannel nightgown. She wasn't getting back to sleep in a hurry, and there was no way she could just lie there. Reaching for her terry robe, she flung it on, deciding to go downstairs and get a book from the well-stocked shelves in the lounge where they had been sitting that evening.

Every slight creak of the old oak boards under her bare feet cut like a knife through the thick blanket of silence as she tiptoed down the stairs. No streetlights penetrated the closed curtains and the downstairs lay in inky blackness. It certainly was dark down there.

Come on, Julia, don't be silly. With that comforting thought she rounded the newel post and made her way toward the lounge, guided by the dim red glow in the hearth. The dying embers gave off just enough light for her to make out the outlines of the furniture.

After fumbling around on the walls by the door, looking for the light switch, she gave up and went over to the bookcase. Her heart was beating uncomfortably fast and she felt an increasingly urgent need to get back upstairs to her nice, safe, brightly lit bedroom. Served her right for listening to ghost stories right before bed. Suddenly she felt ten years old again, creeping around in the dark on Halloween and scaring herself to death.

She could blame that story for her dream or, rather, nightmare. *Nightmare?* her conscience chided her. *Don't pretend you didn't enjoy it.* Just thinking about that kiss made the sensation come back so vividly she could almost feel his warm breath on her face. She shivered. God, it was cold down here. Pulling out a paperback at random, she clutched it to her breast and started for the door. Out of the corner of her eye she caught a flash of gold in the darkness behind the rocking chair where Amy had sat.

She turned her head and peered into the shadows. In the dull glow of the embers she thought she caught a glimpse of gold buttons on scarlet. Every hair on the nape of her neck stood on end as her flesh prickled and her mouth went dry.

After the first second of paralysis, a surge of adrenalin went shuddering through her. Without another conscious thought she dashed out of the room in a headlong rush for the stairs, her heart leaping out of her chest.

Stumbling over something in the pitch-black hall, she fell against the bottom step, banging her shin on the bare wood. Heedless of the crippling pain, she scrambled up the stairs on her hands and knees in sheer panic.

Regaining her feet on the landing, she dashed up the next flight, flew around the corner, and cannoned into a hard body with a resounding thud. The impact sent her sprawling backwards to land on the floor, dazed and shaken.

"Julia! Are you all right?"

Martin's familiar voice cut through the darkness. Then she felt his hands on her waist and shoulder as he helped her to her feet. She realized she was still trembling when his arms went around her and pulled her against him.

"What were you doing running around like that in the dark?"

His husky voice had softened, and she found it difficult to answer as she became aware of muscled flesh against her lips. She could feel the rapid thud of his heartbeat beneath her palms, the soft hairs tickling her nostrils as she inhaled the fresh scent of soap on his bare skin. The dream came flooding back in vivid detail, and she gently pushed against his chest to break free of him.

"I'm fine now, Martin . . . please let me go," she murmured, her words muffled against his skin.

He slowly released her and allowed her to move away slightly. Opening her bedroom door, he took hold of her arm and steered her through, following her into the lighted room.

He closed the door behind him with a soft click and turned her to face him, capturing her upper arms in his strong fingers. "Now what's this all about?"

Julia blinked. He was surprisingly solid and muscular for a man who looked so slim when clothed. She took in the strong curve of his broad shoulders, the powerful expanse of his chest, lightly sprinkled with golden hair. Her eyes slowly, involuntarily, drifted down his bare torso, skin gleaming in the lamplight, over the firm plane of his stomach. Her gaze dropped inexorably down past the point where the hair swirled around his navel to the tan corduroy pants, sitting low on his lean hips, and the partially zipped fly revealing a hint of dark blond curls. She gulped, then swallowed hard over the lump in her throat as her eyes shot back up to meet his.

Martin gazed at her small, pale face surrounded by a fetching tumble of auburn curls. Until today he'd never seen her with her hair down before, literally or figuratively speaking. Yet all day long a vision had kept intruding on his thoughts, the sight of Julia in that outrageously sexy lingerie, blowing all his preconceptions to smithereens.

What sort of a woman was this? He'd had her pegged as an uptight prude, right down to her sensible underwear, yet there she had stood like something out of an erotic fantasy, those endless legs inspiring all kinds of wayward thoughts.

And if that wasn't enough to convince him there was more to her than met the eye, there had been the feel of her soft, slender curves in his arms a few minutes ago. So warm, so feminine, sending a tremor of unexpected desire racing through him.

He didn't usually pursue women, especially those who were clearly unimpressed with him. He'd never had to. But now he was definitely intrigued, he wanted to know more. It was almost laughable. And just yesterday he thought he had Julia Bennett all figured out.

He was watching her. She gazed into the unreadable blue depths and saw him making his own inventory. She could just imagine what she must look like, her long hair a tangled mess, her faded old flannel nightgown showing beneath her open robe and her face bare of makeup.

This had better not become a habit. Every time he'd been in her room, one of them had been practically naked. At least she now felt secure in the knowledge that whatever else he embellished, he was, in fact, a real blond.

"Julia!" he barked, giving her a shake. "What happened?"

Startled into realizing she'd been standing gawking at him for a full minute, she felt a burning red flush wash over her entire body. What was the matter with her? You'd think she'd never been rescued from a ghost by a half-naked man at three o'clock in the morning.

"Nothing . . . nothing at all. I just tripped and fell."

How could she possibly tell him the truth? He was the last person on earth she would supply with that kind of ammunition, especially after the way she'd scoffed at the whole idea of ghosts. He would never let her live something like this down.

"I don't believe you. You were terrified."

She pulled away out of his grasp. "Well, of course, I was terrified. I didn't expect you to be standing there."

She hugged herself and rubbed her arms. Now that the fear had subsided she was beginning to feel chilled again and extremely stupid.

"Who were you expecting? . . . Captain Fairfax?"

Julia squirmed away from his questioning look. "Don't be ridiculous."

Martin suddenly let out a loud burst of laughter.

"Would you please keep it down," she hissed, mortified by his amusement. "You'll wake Amy, if she isn't up already."

"I doubt that she'd hear us. We've got this wing all to ourselves." He tried unsuccessfully to sober up. "You spooked yourself, didn't you?" He wagged a knowing finger in her face, laughing at her.

"I did not." She grabbed his finger in annoyance, then quickly changed her mind at the feel of his warm, hard flesh and let it go. "I merely tripped and fell."

"Like hell you did. You came tearing up those stairs like some wailing banshee was at your heels. I thought you didn't believe in ghosts."

She rewarded his teasing with a sugary sweet smile. "I'm so happy to provide you with this opportunity for fun. Now, if you've had enough, do you mind leaving? I'd like to go to bed."

"Not at all." His smile openly mocked her as he sauntered over to the door and swung it open. "The offer still stands, you know." He paused with his hand on the knob and glanced back at her. "You can snuggle up to me if you want. I could protect you from that ghostly womanizer." The smile deepened to a grin and he waggled his eyebrows in an exaggerated leer.

"Like I said before, I'd rather take my chances with the ghost."

He stood facing her in the doorway, hands on his hips. "Do you want to go down and tell him that?"

She shut the door on his mocking grin, scrambled under the warm quilt, and heard him chuckling, then his door closing and silence.

Damn that man. Ever since this truce she'd been more aware of him than she wanted to be. And his behavior toward her was different, teasing, almost . . . flirtatious. But no, she shifted restlessly, it had to be her imagination.

Julia plumped up her pillow with several vicious jabs and flopped over onto her stomach, then a few moments later rolled onto her back again. This was no good.

She sat up and looked for the book she'd risked her life to get, then remembered where she'd left it—lying at the bottom of the stairs where she'd tripped. And no power on earth could get her back down those stairs before morning.

What was she worried about anyway? Just because he'd been amusing himself at her expense didn't mean his opinion of her had changed. And even though she'd seen unexpected facets to Martin, all the things she disliked about him still remained. Reassured that the world was still spinning on its axis, and all things were as they should be, she turned out the light.

FOUR

Julia slid into the red vinyl booth beside the plate glass window that gave her a clear view of Queen Street. Eight in the morning and rush hour in Niagara-on-the-Lake. She must have seen as many as five cars in her ten-minute walk through the quiet streets of the historic little town to June's Diner.

Of course, she could have eaten breakfast at the George, but that would have meant facing *him*. No, she'd rather brave the icy wind than try to choke down her meal under the mockery in his translucent blue eyes.

After the embarrassment of the night before, she wanted to put off their meeting until later in the day. With any luck he'd have contracted amnesia and forgotten about the incident, although it would take her several lifetimes to achieve the same blissful state.

And she didn't sneak out of the hotel. That was something people did to avoid paying their bills. She had merely ducked into the hall closet when she heard him come whistling down the stairs and lurked between the coats until he had safely passed. It would have been all right if Amy hadn't come along and opened the door. With any luck the woman would just consider her a harmless eccentric.

But she felt more like a lunatic. Replacing the book in its spot on the shelf that morning, she discovered her ghost of the night before had been nothing more than an old red blazer hanging on a hook by the fireplace.

"Wanna menu?" A buxom waitress with two long blond braids plunked a red leatherette folder down in front of her, then poured steaming coffee into her cup. "Just here for the day?"

Glancing up from the menu, Julia noticed the spark of curiosity in the waitress's eyes. In the mid-winter doldrums any stranger must be an object of interest.

"No, I'm staying at the George for a week or so. Writing an article about the town."

The woman's face lit up with a warm smile, revealing a slight gap between her two front teeth. She had the look of a wholesome farm girl, Julia thought, the kind you saw advertising Danish cheese.

"Wow . . . isn't that interesting. Where are you from?"

"Toronto." The smell of frying bacon was making her hunger pangs worse. "I'd like the Fruitpicker's Special, please." Julia smiled, closed the menu, and handed it to the waitress.

"One Fruitpicker's Special, Charlie!" she yelled toward the kitchen, then turned back to Julia. "So, you're from Toronto. I always wanted to live in Toronto, but my fiancé hates it. He lived there once, you know, but he says it's way too crowded and dirty." Her wide brown eyes were eloquent with disappointment. "Funny thing is, he's something in your line. He wanted to work as a reporter with one of the big newspapers," she sighed, "but all he could get was a job delivering them."

Julia choked on her coffee and looked up to see if

the woman was being sarcastic, but all she could see was artless naivete on her broad, flat features.

"I wish he could have thought of something else he'd like to do there, but he hated it too much. He came back here and now he works at the *Gleaner*—that's our local paper."

"Well, isn't that interesting," Julia responded. "I'll have to pick up a copy."

"Oh, there's never very much in it."

Once again she seemed completely unconscious of how her words sounded. Julia had to smother a smile as the waitress continued.

"It's pretty boring stuff except when the theater people are in town. But I'd still like to try living in Toronto. All the shops and the bright lights. It's so dull round here, especially at this time of year."

"It's only an hour and a half away. Surely you could always go in for the day or the weekend."

"I guess." She sighed and flipped back a blond braid. "I wanted to take a secretarial course there, but Eric wouldn't let me. He says that his wife won't have to work. But I'm not his wife yet. I'm still waiting."

Julia restrained herself from pointing out that waitressing was most definitely work. "Well, I think Niagara-on-the-Lake is a charming little town," she said diplomatically. "It's so quaint and peaceful."

"That's because you don't live here. Eric says there are so many rich snobs around here they should call it Niagara-on-the-Make."

Julia burst out laughing.

"No, really, it's true," the waitress said with a wide-eyed innocence that seemed unreal in a woman who looked to be in her mid-thirties. "But he wouldn't put that into the newspaper because he could get into big trouble."

"Your number two's ready!" yelled a disembodied voice from the kitchen.

The woman hurried away in a whirl of blond braids, and Julia sipped her coffee, grinning from ear to ear. Was there something in the water here?

She glanced around the long, narrow diner at the few patrons eating in silence and staring at their newspapers. "Established 1958" it said at the top of the menu, and it looked as though they hadn't changed the decor since opening day. The long laminated counter, the green linoleum floor, the inevitable dusty rubber plant in the corner. Even down to the little table jukeboxes with a repertoire of songs that didn't appear to go past 1965, Julia noticed, flipping through the one at her table.

Gazing idly out the window, she suddenly spotted the wretch who had kept her awake for the better part of the night. Shoulders hunched against the freezing wind, Martin came hurrying down Queen Street and was just drawing level with the diner.

Seized with sudden panic, she grabbed the only thing on the table, a flier advertising the Wednesday senior's special. Trying to hide behind a three-by-five piece of card proved worse than useless, so she threw it down and ducked forward behind the tiny jukebox, pretending to study the song list. It was either that or diving under the table. But it was too late.

Out of the corner of her eye she saw the blue parka stop outside the frosty window right beside her, then heard a tap on the glass. Wanting to ignore him but knowing that would be impossible, she let her gaze travel up the long zipper of the coat to meet the blatant amusement in his eyes. With a brazen smile he pointed inside, then moved past the window.

She sat there stirring cream into her coffee, resigned to her fate. She couldn't even drum up any good old-fashioned resentment for all the trouble she'd taken sneaking out, giving Amy Balfour the impression she was a raving lunatic. A gust of cold air whirled around her feet as the door opened and he appeared by her table.

"Good morning." He looked disgustingly bright and cheerful, his lean cheeks flushed from the cold, his hair windblown and even more messy than usual.

"It was." For the second time that morning she'd acted like an idiot because of this man. Thank God he hadn't been the one to discover her lurking behind the coats.

"Brrr . . ." He rubbed his hands together. "No wonder I can't get warm in here. In that sort of mood, are we? I suspected something was wrong when I saw you lock yourself in the closet this morning."

Julia snatched up her cup, spilling the coffee.

Martin shook his head and pulled out a handful of paper napkins from the dispenser on her table. "Oh, Julia, you *are* having a bad morning."

She grabbed the napkins out of his hand. "Give those to me and go away." She mopped up the coffee.

"Well really, old girl, I was merely trying to help."

"Don't 'old girl' me! And I don't need your help, thank you."

As if she wasn't flustered enough already, when she looked up at him all she could see was his sculpted torso gleaming in the lamplight, those lean hips barely clothed. It was more than she could cope with first thing in the morning, before she'd even had her breakfast.

"Does this mean you don't want me to join you?"

She narrowed her eyes in reply and Martin clearly got the message. With a wicked chuckle, he took a stool at the counter.

Pulling out her notebook, Julia tried to concentrate on her "To Do" list but found it impossible. What had happened to her? Ever since coming to Niagara-on-the-Lake, her behavior had resembled something out of *I Love Lucy*. But then she'd never been faced with a man who thought nothing of crawling through a bedroom window because he wanted to talk to her.

From beneath her lashes she watched that impossible man swiveling back and forth on the squeaky stool, his discarded parka on the seat beside him. Her gaze slid down the bulky gray sweater to his well-worn jeans and the way they hugged those slim hips and lean, muscular thighs.

"Wanna menu?"

"No need . . ." Martin leaned forward to read the name tag on the waitress's pink polyester uniform. ". . . Trudi." He smiled, turning the full power of his charm on his unsuspecting victim, and rattled off an order for bacon and eggs.

Trudi might have been vivacious before, but now her beaming face positively sparkled. She dashed off to the kitchen, reappearing with Julia's order and placing the steaming plate in front of her with a quick smile, then sped back to the counter without a word. Julia heaved a sigh as she tucked into her breakfast. Once again another fatal blow to her ego, deposed of her "interesting newcomer" status in the diner.

Quietly amused, she watched Trudi pour Martin's coffee. The waitress's eyes kept darting from the cup to his face. Then she retreated to the far end of the counter and stood staring at him, clearly fascinated. Oblivious to his conquest, Martin leaned on one elbow and read the newspaper while waiting for his meal.

Trudi disappeared into the kitchen. When she returned a few moments later with Martin's plate, Julia choked on the sip of coffee she had just taken. The waitress had undone the two top buttons on her uniform, making it hard to ignore her generously rounded bosom. It was easy to see who she was out to impress.

Suddenly Julia flashed back to the moment Martin had crawled in her bedroom window and seen her practically naked, her slender, small-breasted body clad only in the briefest lace underwear. And for one insane moment she wondered how she would fare in comparison to Trudi's more voluptuous curves.

Trudi carefully laid out Martin's flatware and placed his breakfast before him, leaning as far forward as the counter would allow. He looked up with a smile of thanks. Then Julia saw the smile freeze on his face and his eyes widen, then blink in disbelief when they rested on the waitress's cleavage, mere inches away.

"Is there anything else I can get you?" Trudi breathed down at him in what Julia could only assume was her best Marilyn Monroe.

"No thanks," he smiled dazedly up at her. "I think this is about all I can handle for breakfast."

Julia coughed and choked on her bacon, struggling hard to suppress the urge to laugh. Martin looked over at her and she was amazed to see a flush spreading along his cheekbones. He was actually blushing. If his reaction weren't so funny, she might have felt sorry for him.

Suddenly Trudi gasped, her eyes riveted on the window, then turned and scurried back into the kitchen. Julia looked around to see a man glaring in through the plate glass, his round face as red as the curly hair on his head.

A second later the man entered the diner and walked past her to the next booth, aiming a murderous glare at the back of Martin's head.

He appeared to be in his early thirties, she guessed, and was of medium height and somewhat plump, even without the voluminous tweed topcoat he pulled off and threw down on the banquette.

Trudi reemerged with her buttons demurely fastened and a jug of coffee in her hand. She walked over to his table with a look of defiant bravado, said "Morning, Eric," and poured him his coffee before scooting back to the counter.

Ahh . . . this must be the fiancé. The man plunked himself down on the vinyl seat with a glare at Trudi's retreating back and snapped open his paper, clearing his throat with a note of outrage. The situation was becoming more interesting by the minute.

To add insult to injury, Martin was chatting with Trudi, telling her all about his work, blithely unaware of the raw, primitive passions he seemed to be arousing in the other man's breast or the dazed fascination on Trudi's face.

But her boyfriend looked as if he was on the verge of grabbing Martin by the scruff of the neck and hauling him outside. Julia chewed on her lip. The rising tension had become almost unbearable. She could tell by the bright pink splotches on her fleshy cheeks that Trudi was only too aware of it, despite her bedazzled state. The only person who remained in blissful ignorance was Martin.

Perhaps some soothing music would help defuse the situation. Julia flipped through the song list until "What A Wonderful World" by Louis Armstrong caught her eye. Just what the situation needed, something sweet and heartwarming. She dug a quarter out of her pocket, put it in, and pushed the buttons.

Mick Jagger's salacious growl came blaring out from the distorted speakers with the heavy guitar sounds of "Let's Spend the Night Together." Julia nibbled at her toast and stared hard out the window, dangerously close to maniacal giggling. How could she have pressed the wrong buttons? But it was too late now.

Glancing over at Martin, she caught his surprise, then the dawning amusement lighting his eyes. The conceited swine. He'd better not think that song was an invitation. He had about as much chance of spending the night with her as a snowball in hell.

Besides anything else, he might not survive the

morning, judging by the furious face of the man in the next booth.

Mercifully unaware, Martin leaned forward confidentially, laying on the suave English charm with a trowel. ". . . you know, Trudi love, you might be able to help me with my research."

Julia rolled her eyes and finished up her scrambled eggs. She couldn't stand it anymore. If she didn't leave now, she'd rupture something.

Making a hurried exit, she sped down Queen Street, then suddenly came to a dead stop.

Where was she going?

A million unanswered questions bounced around in her brain and she felt a terrifying sense of confusion. What was she going to do with this story? It was all very well to insist she could handle it, but she'd never tackled something with such limitless scope, and now there was no one to give her direction except herself. Had she bitten off more than she could chew? The enormity of the task hit her and she felt swamped by rising panic.

Hold on there, Julia old girl. Drat! She was even starting to sound like that infuriating man. In just one day he had her so rattled and confused she was losing her focus.

Now. What angle did she want to take? What was the most important aspect of the story for her?

Once again she could see those bleached bones lying on the table in the museum lab. She had been almost repelled by the way the doctor had pointed out signs of scurvy and old wounds on the skeletons. She'd been so clinical, when all Julia could think of was—these were people. They had lived and died in anonymity and their families had never known what had happened to them.

She thought of the ghost story Amy had told and how keenly she had felt that long ago sorrow. She thought of all those who had died in the war and those who had survived. What of old Jebediah Balfour? The chimney he had built still stood two centuries later.

So often, in the accounts she'd read of this particular war, it seemed to her the ordinary people were forgotten. The events surrounding them took on more importance than the people who had shaped them.

Of course! It was as if a mist had cleared from her mind. That's what her story would be about. People. And she knew exactly where to start. She turned and headed swiftly down the sidewalk.

All alone in the small back room of the library, Julia sat at one end of the reading table engrossed in *Strolling Through Our Town,* a charming book written by a local antiquarian at the turn of the century.

Absorbed as she was, she became aware of the librarian's high-pitched voice approaching down the corridor, outside the slightly open door facing her.

"Yes, the military records are in there, too, on microfiche, along with land grants, newspaper files, and all kinds of town records. You'll also find our collection of rare books and historical journals. Strangely enough, you're the second person I've had in today asking about that information. In fact, I believe the young lady is still in there."

It wasn't hard to guess who else was on the other side of the door. Julia carefully put down her pen, folded her hands on the table, and waited for him to walk into the room.

A moment later Martin's tall, slim form filled the doorway. She knew he would be expecting to see her sitting there. What would she see on his face? That mockery, that devilish humor he loved to employ to make her ill at ease? Would he be put out because she was there first?

But she was completely unprepared for the dazzling

smile that lit his face, without a trace of artifice, as if he were genuinely pleased to see her.

His smile filled her with warmth, like the hot summer sun soaking into her bones. She responded, smiling back spontaneously. At that moment he made her feel as if, of all the people who could have been in the room, she was the one he most wanted to see.

"Please continue with your research. I didn't mean to disturb you." Something about his soft, slightly husky voice did strange things to her nerves.

Martin threw his knapsack on the table, hung his parka on the back of a chair, and went over to the bookshelves ranged along the wall to her left. He began perusing the titles, whistling softly. She looked down at her book again, but her gaze was drawn to him continually. Suddenly he stopped whistling and turned around. Quickly she dropped her eyes to her book, but not quite fast enough.

"Julia . . ." he said slowly. "You're not cheating and trying to see what I'm choosing, are you?"

"Of course I'm not." She felt her cheeks grow warm and glanced up to see the telltale teasing glint in his eye.

From then on she kept her eyes strictly on the page in front of her, but none of the words seemed to be sinking in. All her senses were acutely tuned to his movements in the small room until he finally plunked a pile of books on the end of the table, sat down, leaned over, and pushed the door shut.

"It's very distracting having all that noise."

Not nearly as distracting as his presence, even more so in the sudden quiet. Her breathing sounded unnaturally loud. She even imagined she could hear her heart beating. She quickly looked down again, then darted a look toward him.

He sat with one elbow propped on the table, stroking a finger over his bearded chin, and opened the top book in his pile. She didn't care for beards, or facial hair of any kind on men. And she didn't like long, messy hair like Martin's that flopped into his eyes and brushed the top of his sweater at the back. So why was she starting to think that on him they didn't look so bad?

The next time she glanced toward him he had rested his cheek on his fist and was staring at her, with a provocative look in his eyes she found intensely disconcerting. He held her gaze until she couldn't stand it anymore.

"Okay," she blurted out. "What is it?"

"Did you know that your sweater is exactly the same color as your eyes? What do you call that color anyway, that bluey-purple color?"

"Violet."

"I suppose you must have chosen that shade on purpose. Now why did I never notice what lovely eyes you have, Julia?"

Was this the man who only twenty-four hours ago had been so denigrating about her lack of charm?

"Umm . . . I suppose you never really looked before." She hoped to heaven he couldn't tell how much his compliment affected her. Considering the source, she felt unreasonably flattered.

"Well, I'm looking now." His gaze slowly traveled over her face, resting on her mouth for a moment, then back up to her eyes with such frank and open sensuality it took her breath away.

"I wish you wouldn't, because I really have to get down to work." The words came out in a rush. "It's very distracting having someone sitting there staring." Not to mention the effect it was having on her heartbeat.

He shrugged and opened another of the volumes in front of him. With a tiny feeling of relief, Julia forced her attention back to her own book, but after a few minutes her eyes strayed over toward him again, only to find his gaze riveted on her once more. His scrutiny was so blatant that she could do nothing but stare back, almost holding her breath, waiting for what he would come out with next.

"I was just wondering, do you always wear your hair tied back? I was thinking last night that all those auburn curls looked very appealing tumbled around your face."

Before she could check the gesture, Julia's hand flew self-consciously to the French braid that hung down her back. The movement brought a small smile to Martin's eyes. That devil! He was playing some kind of little game with her.

Since when did she have trouble handling compliments? Most social situations found her cool and composed, more than capable of holding her own. But this man had her behaving with less confidence than she had had at sixteen. This was useless. She couldn't sit here a moment longer.

"I think I'll work on this later," she began in the most nonchalant tone she could dredge up. "There's something else I have to do right now." Gathering up her notebook and papers, she headed for the door.

As it swung shut behind her, she heard his soft, husky chuckle and groaned silently. *Julia Bennett, you are a prize sap!* He had her figured as an uptight prude he could scare off by a little outrageous flirting and it had worked. Well, if he ever pulled a stunt like that again, she'd know exactly how to deal with it.

FIVE

The glass display cases in the small museum held the history of Niagara in microcosm. Julia walked slowly over the creaking pine boards, looking at the carefully tagged and labeled exhibits, trying to imagine the settlers and soldiers who had held these things in their hands. Everything from pistols and sabers to everyday objects like teapots and china dolls.

She paused to take a closer look at a display of uniforms from the War of 1812 and caught sight of a tall, blond figure standing behind her, reflected in the glass.

"What kept you?" she said without turning around, her voice tinged with the faintest touch of sarcasm. "I've been here at least ten minutes."

Maybe finding him in the bookstore had been a coincidence. And when he waltzed into the Old Niagara Fudge Shop two minutes behind her, maybe he really had been overcome with the irresistible urge for chocolate almond fudge. But now she knew for sure he was deliberately following her, and she didn't have to look too far to discover his reasons.

All she had to do was stay cool and unconcerned, Julia resolved as she turned to face him, then instantly wished she hadn't when she saw the tantalizing smile playing around his lips. She watched his gaze trace over her close-fitting black jodhpurs and violet sweater with the awful sensation that he was looking through them to her body beneath. A body she could feel glowing with heat.

Her cheeks burning, she saw his smile widen to a grin. She looked down at herself to see what could be wrong, then back up to his face.

"Okay. I give up. What is it?"

He stepped closer, until his coat brushed against hers, and looked down into the next display case. Julia followed his gaze to an array of elaborately boned, old-fashioned corsets.

"I was just thinking how much I prefer your taste in lingerie to this." His voice softened to a low, seductive murmur as he leaned slightly toward her. "Tell me, do you always wear peach?"

With an exasperated groan she pushed past him and rushed toward the exit. In retrospect, he had been so much easier to cope with when he'd treated her like the ice maiden he thought her.

Across the water, the gray stones of old Fort Niagara sharpened into clarity as she focused and clicked the shutter. Lowering her camera, Julia caught a glimpse of a figure on the other side of the small gazebo, close to the edge of the embankment bordering the river. After a moment she realized it was Martin, also taking a picture of the fort guarding the American side.

This *was* a very small town. Much too small. She shook her head and began to turn away when Martin, who had been moving forward, suddenly dropped out of sight. For one frozen moment she stood staring at the spot where he had been, then began to run.

Her heart racing, adrenalin rushing through her veins, Julia felt sick with terror. In the frigid, fast-flowing waters of the Niagara River even a strong swimmer couldn't survive more than a few minutes at this time of year.

Reaching the bank, she looked over the edge to see Martin sitting on the narrow strip of damp sand five feet below, dusting off his parka. She stared at him in amazement.

"Are you all right?"

He looked up at Julia's anxious face, her cheeks flushed from running, and shot her a sheepish grin. "I'm fine, just overstepped my mark."

He'd seen a lot of expressions on her face when she looked at him, usually anger or annoyance or downright indifference, most of the time, but never such unwonted concern.

"What else is new?" She started to laugh and held out her hand as he started to get to his feet.

He hesitated for a moment, surprised at the way her laughter filled him with sudden, bubbling exhilaration, then put his hand in hers, enjoying the feel of her long, slender fingers closing around his own. He let her help him up, wishing he could continue holding her hand, but she released him as he scrambled up the loose, sandy soil of the bank, back onto the grass.

He grinned. "You're probably one of those people who laugh at practical jokes, like pulling chairs out from under people."

God, you twit, that was a stupid thing to say. But she was so unexpected, and what she was doing to him was so unexpected, he was in danger of becoming mesmerized by the provocative laughter in those wonderful eyes.

Why had he never noticed until today? He'd always thought her eyes were blue. Just plain blue. Right now they were a lovely translucent violet and he'd be just as happy staring at them all day long. If he wasn't careful, he'd keep on saying the first thing that came into his head and then he'd be in real trouble.

Julia laughed again. "Well, it serves you right. You've been following me around town all morning trying to make me feel uncomfortable."

And she had no idea how much worse he'd tried to make it. It hadn't been a coincidence Amy happened to open that closet door this morning. Only an untimely phone call from Roger had prevented him from enjoying Julia's embarrassment. Ah, well. The best laid plans . . .

". . . And don't deny you've been pretending to flirt with me in an attempt to embarrass me." She bit her lip, suddenly serious. "Well, it worked, you have embarrassed me . . ." Surprised by her own admission, she looked away in confusion.

"But I haven't been pretending."

The caressing quality in his soft voice brought her gaze back to his face, and the intimate way he looked into her eyes made her feel a slow warmth curling deep down inside her. Her heart was having trouble beating. Suddenly it became very important to distance herself from him so she could catch her breath.

She tried to sound matter-of-fact, but her voice stumbled, devoid of conviction. "Well, I'm . . . I'm warning you, it's not going to work anymore. So . . . so just stay out of my way."

She turned abruptly and fled. *Julia, you're running away*. She was not. Just making a strategic retreat. How her father would have snorted if he'd heard that weak excuse from one of his soldiers. But the major hadn't met Martin Taylor.

And for the rest of the day he did stay out of her way.

He didn't show up for lunch at the diner, although she wished that he had. Then she would have been spared Trudi's endless stream of personal questions about him. The only one she felt comfortable answering was the first. No, she wasn't his girlfriend. After that the floodgates had opened. Julia had been intensely relieved to see the fiancé walk in.

She could tell Trudi didn't believe her protestations that she didn't know Martin that well. And she had to restrain herself from laughing when Trudi had told her with childlike simplicity that she understood why Julia would want to keep such a dish to herself.

She caught no sight of Martin at the fort and not even a hint of him at the old parish church. It was as if he'd left town. But perversely, instead of being glad for his absence, Julia became even more edgy. What was he up to now?

She had to stop being such a neurotic and get on with her work. A stray gust of wind picked up last year's dead leaves and swirled them round her feet as she walked briskly across the deserted park. A few small flakes of snow drifted down. Except for the rustling of the dry leaves it was very quiet, so quiet she could easily imagine the peaceful little town as it might have been two hundred years ago. She looked up at the dark, bare branches of the old oaks above her head, silhouetted against the lowering pewter sky. Had any of these trees been here then? Had Sarah Balfour or Captain Fairfax paused beneath their shade?

Back through the center of town and a couple of blocks off the main street, she returned to the nineteenth-century red-brick schoolhouse, now the museum, and headed straight for the wing housing the archives. The handwritten sign on the door had said "Back at three." It was now five past.

A swinging gate, set into a tall dividing wall, led into a small room lined with glass-fronted bookcases. Seated at the pine table, in front of a dilapidated cardboard box full of old documents and photographs, was the young man from the diner.

Julia paused, feeling suddenly awkward. "Excuse me, but I'm here to see the archivist?"

He blinked up at her in surprise, then his eyes hardened a little in recognition. "Well, you've found him. I'm Eric Galway."

He radiated wariness and more than a trace of hostility. She summoned her biggest and friendliest smile.

"My name is Julia Bennett." She held out her hand as he stumbled to his feet reluctantly.

"Yes, I noticed you and your . . . friend in the diner this morning. My fiancée tells me you're journalists from Toronto. I believe you've already met Trudi."

"Yes, and she's charming."

He sniffed. "She tells me that you and your colleague are working together on a story about our town."

"We're both here working on stories," she paused, wondering how to make the situation clear, "but definitely *not* together."

"Oh . . . I see." As he assimilated the information, he seemed to thaw slightly. "And how can I help you, Miss Bennett?"

"I need some information about the War of 1812." She needed to break the ice a little more, so she played a hunch. "As the man responsible for safeguarding the town's heritage, you must be quite an expert on its history."

He blinked twice, then a pleased smile broke out on his freckled face, and she knew she'd hit pay dirt. With a self-important little cough, he straightened his navy cardigan and listened as she went on to explain her assignment.

". . . and I'm particularly looking for human-interest stories. First-person accounts of events that may not be widely known. Actually, Amy Balfour told me about an incident that's exactly the kind of thing I want to use." She went on to tell him Captain Fairfax's story and confessed with a blush her own imaginary run-in with his ghost.

He snorted. "Amy tells that old story to anyone who'll listen."

There was now a touch of amused condescension in his manner. Nothing like disclosing a little fallibility to make the other person relax, Julia thought with relief and made a noncommittal response.

"Well, let's see now." He rubbed his chubby hands together and scanned the crowded shelves. "I'm sure I can find you plenty of material. Well-documented stories, not just embroidered family legends. We don't get too many people through here with a real interest in the war, but I myself have made an extensive study, particularly as it pertains to our geographical location."

She had struck gold. In his pedantic, laborious way Eric inundated her with facts while he opened up the glass doors and pulled out one book after another from the shelves. Before she knew it, he had sat her down at one end of the table with stacks of volumes.

He licked his pale, thin lips. "When it comes to my favorite topic, I'm more than happy to help a fellow professional." He responded to her puzzled look. "I publish the *Niagara Gleaner*, our local newspaper."

His slightly pompous air amused her, and even more so when she thought of Trudi's artless comment that nobody was very interested in the paper.

"I just squeeze in the archival work when I can," he continued. "Fortunately, I have the expertise to ensure our town's history is preserved correctly."

Julia schooled herself to look properly impressed.

She spent the next hour and a half poring through musty old township records and the writings of the amateur historians who had established the museum. Suddenly a passage in one of the nineteenth-century journals caught her eye.

"Hey . . . listen to this." She sat up excitedly and

Eric lifted his head from the pile of documents he had gone back to cataloging. "Whilst exchanging pleasantries with an elder of our town, he chanced to impart to me a legend of the American war which he knew from his father had its basis in fact. It seems that during the hostilities a paywagon carrying silver destined to pay the American militia disappeared under mysterious circumstances from the American side of the river. Townsfolk whispered that it had been brought over to the Canadian side by treasonous American officers in a conspiracy with their British counterparts, and aided by a notorious black marketeer, a scurrilous knave who profited from human misery."

Julia swiftly turned the page, then flipped it back again. "I can't believe it. Not another word about this story." And there was something naggingly familiar about it. "Do you know anything about this, Eric?"

"No . . . No, I don't. What book is that in? I don't remember coming across that before."

She held up the heavy volume so that he could see the spine. At that moment the door opened and Martin strolled in, then stopped short at the sight of her. Surely he couldn't be surprised to see her.

"Can I help you?" Eric's frigid voice sent the clear message that he wasn't interested in helping the other man anywhere but back out again, preferably with a good swift kick.

Martin turned to him with an unabashed smile. "I'm interested in any material you have relating to the War of 1812."

"I'm afraid the material in here is too old and valuable to be handled."

For a moment Martin stared pointedly at the books piled up in front of Julia. She could see he was puzzled by Eric's hostility. In the diner that morning he had missed all those murderous glances directed at the back of his head.

"I see. Well, then . . . perhaps you can tell me where to find the information I'm looking for."

"There are microfiche copies of all this material at the library . . . but that section's closed now."

"And when will it be open?"

Julia could tell from the way he pursed his lips, tightening them at one corner, that Martin's patience was running thin.

"Tuesday, from noon to three," Eric responded.

"Thank you."

Martin looked over at her and Julia raised her shoulders in an imperceptible shrug. She wasn't responsible for Eric's attitude. Yet, by fair means or foul, she seemed to have the edge on him for once and she refused to feel guilty about it.

Hadn't he been the one who said there were no rules? After all, his methods weren't always on the up and up, and if she were going to hold her own against him, she'd better be prepared to fight with whatever weapons were at her disposal. She watched Martin walk out, then turned back to find Eric scowling at the closing door.

It was already quite dark when Julia stepped out into the cold evening and felt the fine, wet snow stinging her cheeks. She shivered and walked quickly through the gate in the white picket fence, then down quiet Castlereagh Street.

As she passed old Memorial Hall next to the museum, a soft whistle lilted through the darkness. She should have known. Hadn't she almost expected it? A figure detached itself from the sheltered gloom of the porch and stepped into the meager pool of light from the street lamp, illuminating Martin's mop of fair hair.

"I have to hand it to you. That was pretty fancy footwork you did in there."

"What are you talking about?" Julia peered up at his face, trying to see his expression, but it lay in shadow. She stamped her feet, feeling the cold begin to penetrate her flat leather boots.

"Don't get me wrong. I'm impressed at how quickly you got that guy on your side. I didn't think you had it in you." Now she detected the edge of cynicism in his voice.

"If you mean what I think you mean, I *don't* have it in me," she tossed off and with a lift of her chin started walking away.

"Come on, Julia. There's nothing wrong with a little creative manipulation," he said behind her. The sly humor in his tone made her wonder if he was laughing at her.

"Is that what you call it? I'd call it plain immoral. Besides, you're the one responsible for Eric's animosity—putting the make on his fiancée," she shot back over her shoulder.

"You've lost me." Taking hold of her arm, he made her pause and face him.

"I'm talking about Trudi at the diner." She began walking again and Martin fell into step beside her on the dark, quiet side street.

"He's her fiancé? Poor Trudi. That bloke looks like he has all the makings of a petty tyrant. I've met his kind before. There are minor officials all over the world who like to cover their insecurity by exaggerating their own importance."

Julia thought of what Trudi had told her about Eric. Martin could very well be right. But she couldn't help feeling sorry for Eric. It must be quite awful being so plagued by a sense of inferiority.

"But that doesn't excuse your behavior."

"My dear girl, in case you didn't notice—and I know very well that you did—I was an innocent victim and it was very cruel of you to laugh at me."

The open humor in his voice made her smile. "I

couldn't help but laugh. Seeing that lethal charm of yours backfire was like poetic justice."

"It can't be that lethal. You never had any trouble resisting it."

The softness in his voice set awareness stirring inside her again. That was the trouble, she wasn't nearly as resistant as she wanted to be, no matter how calculated his attempts to divert her might be. It gave her a small measure of reassurance to know that she had apparently kept her reaction well hidden.

She hardened her tone, determined to keep things in their proper perspective. "I can't say I ever noticed it being turned on for me. And besides, it's hard to be charmed by someone who considers you cold, arrogant, and unapproachable."

"Believe me, I've regretted those words ever since I uttered them."

His sincerity disconcerted Julia so much her steps faltered. "I'm sorry I brought it up. I can't say I'm proud of my part in that conversation either." She picked up her pace again, past the lighted windows of the small framehouses. "Let's concentrate on the problem we have right now. You were right. We *are* going to keep running into each other. It's almost impossible to avoid."

"Wait a minute. I must be hearing things. Did you actually admit I was right about something?"

"I've decided this truce needs a few ground rules," she continued, deliberately ignoring his exaggerated disbelief. "We'll be looking for information in the same places, so I suggest we respect each other's right to work unmolested. Whoever gets there first should be left alone to finish their research. Then it's the other one's turn."

They rounded the corner onto King Street, and the wind off the lake hit Julia full in the face. She huddled down into her wool coat and strode on, wishing she'd worn a hat.

Martin turned his back to the blast and it carried his words to her. "It's a little simplistic, but I'll go for it."

"Let's see you come up with something better."

"You *are* a defensive little thing, Julia. I wasn't criticizing."

He turned and walked close beside her, and she fought down the urge to huddle against him for warmth. At five foot seven it had been a long time since anyone had called her "little."

"All right," he continued. "I agree to your terms, but I think I'm entitled to a show of good faith on your part."

As they stood at the corner of King and Queen, waiting for the line of traffic to pass, she eyed him suspiciously. "What would you suggest?"

"Merely that you stop running away from me like a frightened rabbit." His voice gentled disarmingly, but she hadn't missed the challenging glint that lurked in his crystal blue eyes.

"I didn't run away and I'm not afraid of you." She shuddered and began crossing the street. She didn't like the way this conversation was going.

"Prove it then," he demanded as they reached the other corner. "Stay and have dinner at the George tonight."

Now she liked it even less. "What's that going to prove? We're still on opposite sides and there's a lot at stake as far as I'm concerned."

"You're too suspicious. Did you know that in 1812, in this very town, in this very building as a matter of fact . . ." He stopped and pointed to the nondescript stone facade beside them, and Julia looked up to see the Masonic symbol on the light fixture above the wooden door. ". . . American officers were dining with their British counterparts when war broke out. When the news arrived, they shook hands and toasted each other in a friendly way before they parted to meet later in battle.''

Julia began walking again, quickening her pace until she panted with the exertion, but he caught up effortlessly and strode along beside her.

''I know there must be a point somewhere in this little historical essay. What is it?'' Had the hotel been moved since she left it this morning? It seemed to be taking forever to get there.

''The point is, even if you feel like taking a bayonet to me in the archives, we can at least behave in a civilized manner back at the George. Let's consider it our own private Switzerland, shall we? Neutral territory.''

''Okay,'' she mumbled. Why on earth did she feel this shudder of trepidation? It was only dinner, for heaven's sake. What was there to worry about? Just the two of them, facing each other across a candlelit table in the cozy, romantic isolation of the George.

''Good,'' he smiled. That unholy smile that made the frigid air around her feel suddenly tropical. ''Shall we say dinner at seven?''

SIX

Julia came to an abrupt stop on the threshold of the dining room, and the mink-clad, blue-haired woman behind cannoned into her with an undignified grunt. Mumbling an embarrassed apology, Julia stepped aside, only to be rewarded with a frosty stare. The woman brushed past into the crowded room, a plump, prosperous-looking man in her wake.

Peeking around the doorway, she wondered in growing dismay what had happened to the sleepy little inn. Had it turned into the Imperial Room of the Royal York Hotel in her absence?

The round wooden tables crowding the long room had been transformed by snowy tablecloths laid with crystal and silver, gleaming in the rich golden luster of candlelight. At the far end a blaze roared in the fieldstone hearth, the firelight glowing on the rough-hewn beams of the low ceiling.

And it was full—every table occupied by well-heeled customers in expensive designer casuals. The town had a prosperous air that was hard to miss. She'd noticed the scattering of gracious mansions and estates around the outskirts, but now Julia knew she was in the presence of the privileged elite.

Planning an early night and feeling tired after the long day, she'd slipped gratefully into her comfortable old sweatsuit, never imagining that from Thursday to Saturday the quiet little inn would turn out to be *the* place to dine in the Niagara Peninsula.

Hearing a babble of voices behind her, she turned to see a party of eight approaching the wide doorway. She pressed herself against the doorjamb, feeling incredibly conspicuous, but they passed by without even noticing her. However, the well-tailored, strikingly handsome blond man behind them did notice.

He not only noticed, he held her gaze, walking purposefully toward her with an intimacy in his warm smile that made Julia feel strangely flustered. As if she wasn't used to attracting her fair share of male regard.

But when he got closer, something familiar in his blue eyes caught her attention. Suddenly her heart skipped a beat and her jaw nearly dropped to the ground. It was Martin and he had shaved off his beard.

Unable to believe the change in him, she stared at the lean, well-defined features that had lurked beneath all that hair. The wild man from Borneo had disappeared, and in his place stood this youthful, incredibly good-looking stranger. Much too good-looking for comfort.

"Good evening." His soft, husky voice made the two innocuous words sound like an invitation into bed.

"Hello," Julia croaked from her suddenly dry throat, then swallowed hard, her gaze running over Martin from head to foot, coming back to rest on his smoothly shaven face again. She felt as though her world had just rocked on its heels.

"I'm glad to see all my efforts to make myself presentable to you have been worthwhile."

Her gaze lingered on his mouth for a moment, caught

by the sensual curve of his well-shaped lips as he smiled. She noticed his eyes twinkling with mocking humor at her astonishment. One thing hadn't changed, thank goodness. He was still the same annoying rogue she knew.

"I can't believe you did this all for my benefit." She smiled back at him through slightly narrowed eyes, remembering his shameless behavior in the library.

"Oh, Julia," he laughed, "do you see a communist plot behind every bush?"

She shot him a wry look. "It's safer that way when dealing with you."

Martin shook his head in amusement. "Frankly, I half expected you wouldn't even show up."

Face it, he'd been downright afraid she wouldn't show up. It was a little strange to feel so much anticipation and to know how disappointed he'd feel if she hadn't appeared. "Well, shall we go in?"

He took her arm, but Julia pulled back. "Wait a minute. I can't go in dressed like this."

Tilting his head to one side, he allowed his gaze to roam over her in a leisurely appraisal. The loose green tracksuit hid her curves, but he could visualize them perfectly. And what silky little nothings was she wearing underneath? The prospect tantalized his imagination.

A sudden flush of heat washed over Julia. She felt as if she were standing in front of him naked.

"You look fine to me." He smiled into her eyes, setting off a wild fluttering in the pit of her stomach.

Trying to ignore the disturbing sensation, Julia made her voice brusque. "Look. I'm not going in there dressed like a Queen Street bag lady when you look like you just stepped out of *GQ*. I wouldn't have believed you even owned a suit!"

Where were the old jeans, the baggy corduroy pants? In their place he wore a well-cut navy suit that hung perfectly on his slim, broad-shouldered frame.

"Don't get into a flap, it's the only one I have. And by the way, I happen to like the Queen Street bag lady look."

"You would, considering you usually look like you get your fashion sense from the jungles of Borneo . . . but nevertheless I can't go in there dressed like this. Just look at those people in there."

He glanced into the crowded room with a disdainful grimace. "Yeah . . . they remind me of that Rosedale snob who used to meet you after work. In his three-piece suit and his Jag Sovereign. He looked like the type of guy who'd even have his underwear monogrammed."

Julia suppressed a smile. His succinct description fit Brian all too well. If he were her escort, he'd be insisting she get upstairs and change before anyone else saw her.

"There you are, my dears." Amy suddenly appeared at her elbow in an elegant burgundy dress, looking as regal as her plump, five-foot frame would allow. "I've saved a lovely table for two by the window just for you."

With a resigned shrug Julia followed Amy through the busy dining room, only too aware of Martin beside her, his hand resting on the small of her back. And he was whistling softly under his breath, a vaguely familiar tune. Half-remembered lyrics from a black-and-white musical ran through her head.

". . . Got my top hat . . . got my silk tie . . . all I need now is the girl . . ."

"Is that all it would take? A top hat and a silk tie?"

His words made Julia look up to find him smiling, and she realized she'd sung the lyrics out loud.

"That only happens in the movies."

"You sound disappointed." His voice was soft and intimate beside her ear, and the warm hand resting on the small of her back massaged her ever so slightly. A slow tingling heat radiated from the place where he touched her, cascading down every nerve until her legs felt a little weak.

She quickly looked away and focused her eyes on Amy's plump form ahead, trying to concentrate on anything but the man beside her.

Above the background murmur, tantalizing snippets of conversation met her ears. ". . . so I bought before they announced the merger and the stock went up a hundred points . . . That new spa in Arizona is fabulous, I'm going back next week . . . I picked up five acres, a steal at a million and a half . . ." Yes, this was definitely not the crowd from June's Diner.

A trolley laden with sumptuous desserts blocked their way and they paused to allow the waiter room to maneuver.

Sneaking a glance up at Martin, Julia had to admit he was easily the best-looking man in the room. Wearing a suit had been quite a concession, though Brian would have turned up his distinguished nose at something so obviously off-the-rack. But even Brian's twelve hundred dollar's worth of Italian designer tailoring couldn't give him Martin's air of dashing virility.

Of course, a tie would have been too much to expect. Her gaze lingered a moment too long at the open collar of the pristine white shirt, noticing a few dark golden wisps against his lightly tanned skin.

And his hair. It actually looked as though he'd spent time on it with a brush and a blow dryer so that it waved back, like smooth golden silk, from his broad forehead.

But above all, Julia found her consciousness focused with burning clarity on the pressure of his hand, still resting lightly against the curve of her lower back. She shivered with awareness.

He leaned down toward her. "Stop being so nervous about the way you're dressed or people *will* notice," he said softly.

Julia could feel his warm breath on her cheek. For once he was way off the mark, thank goodness. Who cared if he thought her terminally insecure about her clothes, so long as he didn't guess the real reason for her jitters?

The waiter pushed the trolley out of the way, and as they moved on, Amy said over her shoulder, "I hope you're hungry because the special is rack of lamb tonight, although we have plenty to choose from . . ." She led them to a table for two by a window, tucked into a far corner of the room.

"I'll send the waiter right over," she told them with a smile, before bustling off to greet the newcomers waiting at the door.

Julia took the chair Martin held for her, then watched him slowly lower his lanky frame into the other seat, his eyes never leaving her face.

"When we agreed to have dinner, I had no idea the George would turn out to be the Ritz of the North." Unwilling to hold his gaze, her glance ran over the crowded room. "You didn't say anything about sitting together, and I have to confess I was planning to catch you on a technicality and take another table."

He laughed. "Thanks for being so honest, but I expected as much. I'm beginning to understand what makes you tick."

"If I didn't know better, I'd think you engineered this whole thing." With a wry smile, she shook her head and waved toward the packed tables.

His soft laughter washed over her. "I'm flattered you think I'm so powerful."

"Don't let it go to your head. The word I had in mind was *manipulative*."

He wagged his finger at her with a sly smile. "Switzerland, remember?"

The smile deepened the creases by his mouth and the tiny laugh lines at the corners of his eyes. He really was quite devastatingly attractive, and the realization gave her an uncomfortable jolt. Stricken with self-consciousness, she let her gaze drop to the menu and she greeted the arrival of the fresh-faced young waiter with relief.

He stood waiting, his pencil poised expectantly, and Julia realized she'd been too involved in her surreptitious study of Martin to make any sense of the menu in front of her. She quickly ordered the special and declined a drink, knowing she'd need all her wits about her this evening.

After discussing the various dishes on the menu with the waiter, Martin chose the lamb as well and a beer to go with it. The young man departed, and the silence between them lengthened and grew increasingly awkward, made even more pronounced by the animated buzz of conversation at the surrounding tables.

Julia stared out into the darkness. The snow had stopped and through the bare branches of the trees outside the window a few stars had appeared in the inky black sky. In the distance she could see the yellowish glow of Toronto across the lake. So much safer to study the nonexistent view than look into those disturbing blue eyes she could feel watching her.

How could a superficial change in his appearance affect her like this? But it wasn't that simple, and she knew it. Seeing him in a different way had just shocked her into recognizing something that had been slowly happening ever since they arrived here.

Catching sight of her reflection in the window, she saw what he was seeing and her self-consciousness increased. Could that really be her? She stared at the wide-eyed young woman in sloppy green sweats, gleaming auburn curls escaping from the single French braid that hung down her back. With nervous fingers she tucked the loose strands of hair behind her ears.

"Stop fidgeting," he murmured. "You look fine."

Julia dropped her hands to her lap and leaned back in her chair. "Coming from such an arbiter of style, I find that incredibly unreassuring." But the smile that accompanied her words made him laugh.

"You know, Julia, you worry far too much. About everything. I prefer the way you look right now to those perfect little navy suits and that scraped-back hairdo."

He didn't just prefer it—the contrast had him puzzled and intrigued. Out of her office uniform she seemed so much softer, so different. He hadn't even realized her hair was curly, for God's sake. She usually kept it as disciplined as her demeanor. How could he have let her facade mislead him like that?

"Women have to be conscious of the way they look in business." She looked flustered and didn't quite meet his eyes. "A man can run around looking like an unmade bed, but a woman is always judged on her image."

"So what's yours? Corporate clone?" He was starting to think it was more of a disguise. She wasn't the person he thought she was at all. "You look extremely elegant but so unapproachable. And that's not you at all, is it? Why do you feel the need to look so uptight?"

Julia felt pain and disappointment cut through her like a knife. But why should she care? She already knew his unflattering opinion of her. And she already suspected that his flirtation game was designed to fluster her and throw her off.

Their dinner arrived. Julia unfolded her napkin and gazed down at the steaming plate laid in front of her, inhaling the delicious aroma of roast lamb.

After the waiter left, Martin leaned across the table toward her. The candle illuminated the glint of mischief dancing in his blue eyes as he continued more softly, "However, there is one area of your wardrobe I have no quarrel with."

"Don't you dare mention that!" Julia felt the hot

color rising in her face. Once again in her mind's eye she saw his shocked expression when he crawled in through her window and caught her standing there in her bra and panties. "Switzerland or no Switzerland, I swear I'll strangle you if you bring that up again."

He pushed her plate an inch closer. "For God's sake, eat something. Hunger is making you vicious." He grinned. "Besides, *what* shouldn't I bring up again?"

His innocent act didn't wash for a second. "Look. I know that you know that I know exactly what you mean by that. So don't play dumb with me!"

His grin widened. "What a pithy conversationalist you are, Julia. I do hope your articles are a little less convoluted."

She cut into her lamb with a vengeance. "Did you invite me here just to bait me and make me feel uncomfortable?"

"No . . ." he said slowly. "I didn't. Look, I promise I won't say anything else that could even remotely be considered provocative. Let's pretend we just met. Let's start fresh."

"Let's just eat our dinner."

For a few minutes they ate in awkward silence. The lamb tasted delicious. At any other time she'd be attacking it with relish, but tonight something disturbing had taken away her appetite. The realization that the more time she spent with Martin, the more her awareness and attraction toward him were increasing.

"Come on, eat up," he admonished. "Don't let it get cold."

Julia realized she'd stopped eating and was staring out into the blackness again. She hurriedly sliced into her roast potatoes and gave herself a mental shake. Heaven forbid he should notice any change in her.

"You wouldn't want Amy to think you're not enjoying her wonderful food, would you?" He paused for a bite of lamb. "After all, people come from miles around to dine at the George. Even though we're staying here, I had to do some fast talking to get us a table on such short notice."

Yes, he was good at that, wasn't he, manipulating people to get what he wanted? Had she become a victim, too? Had it just taken a little longer for her to capitulate to his charm along with everyone else?

She bent her head to the food again but noticed his fork remained poised in mid-air. Raising her eyes to his face, she found him watching her intently, his eyes narrowed in speculation.

"Now what?" She couldn't keep the suspicion out of her voice.

"It just occurred to me, I've worked with you for two months and I know nothing about you."

"Perhaps you weren't interested enough to find out. After all, we didn't exactly hit it off, did we?"

"True. But you seem to know far more about me than I do about you. It makes me wonder what sort of deep, dark secrets you're hiding."

"Oh, please . . . spare me the investigative journalist routine. Not everyone is a self-important windbag like you."

He let his fork fall with a clatter. "All right, that's enough."

Heads turned at the next table and Julia shrank down in her chair, torn between an acute attack of the giggles and intense embarrassment. Why did he have to be so conspicuous?

"I really must invoke the Geneva Convention here. There are rules about the fair treatment of prisoners of war and you are subjecting me to cruel verbal abuse."

She burst out laughing at his wounded innocence. "Well, I'm just getting you back for all the fairy tales of yours I've had to listen to. Not to mention the way poor, misguided Eunice is constantly singing your praises."

"If it's any consolation, she's forever telling me what a sweetheart you are and that there's no reason for us not to get along. In fact, we can thank Eunice for our present situation. She offered to book me into a hotel and look what happened."

Julia gaped—and she had accused *him* of causing mischief. "How could she do that to me?"

"I'm glad she did. It's given us an opportunity to get to know each other."

His voice suddenly became serious, as if he really meant it, and Julia felt confused. He seemed genuine and yet . . .

"So tell me, who were you before you became Julia Bennett, girl reporter with a gigantic chip on her shoulder?"

She stiffened and the familiar pain went through her. He was still making fun of her. She had no reason to assume that his disparaging opinion of her had changed completely.

"There's not much to tell," she murmured evasively. It wasn't as if he really cared. "Besides, I wouldn't want to bore you. My life wouldn't hold a candle to some of your exploits, I'm sure."

"Now I'm even more intrigued."

No, he wasn't. He was just trying to pass the time. But she had to admit that it was preferable to eating by herself. In spite of the fact that she suspected he was playing some sort of game, she was glad she came.

"Hey! . . . look who's at the next table. Why it's Captain Fairfax!"

Julia had started up and turned her head to look before she realized what he'd said.

"Just making sure you were awake. You looked like you were either miles away or there was something dodgy about your food."

The corners of his mouth curved with boyish mischief,

and Julia tried unsuccessfully to suppress the smile tugging at her own lips. The man was incorrigible.

The strain of the evening, on top of Martin's transformation into respectability, had been too much for her. There could be no other reasonable explanation for her weird behavior.

He leaned one elbow on the table and rested his chin on his fist, smiling at her in a most disturbing way. "But seriously, you've piqued my curiosity now and I'm warning you I won't rest until I've uncovered your mysterious past."

"Why don't we talk about you instead? It seems to be your favorite topic of conversation."

Her dry comment made him throw back his head and laugh. "My dear girl, I would be incapable of disappointing you."

He took a sip of his beer and she watched in fascination as his tongue darted out to lick the foam off his upper lip. Her gaze dropped sharply to her plate. She had to stop this right now. It was embarrassing, and he was too perceptive not to notice eventually.

He cleared his throat and began portentously, "I was born at a very young age on a cold October day thirty-four years ago on Amblesey, a small island off the west coast of England."

"Wait a minute. Are you leading me on?" This sounded like another tall tale.

"Would I joke about something as momentous as the occasion of my birth?" Julia rolled her eyes and he held up a pacifying hand. "Okay . . . seriously now. I was the oldest of five children, the only son, and—I know this part will make you very happy—a great disappointment to my parents."

She smiled. "I can't say I'm surprised. What awful thing did you do to disappoint them?"

"As the son and heir, I was expected to take over the farm that had been in our family for six generations, but I didn't fancy spending the rest of my life with a herd of sheep."

"A sheep farm? Somehow I can't picture you in such a pastoral setting." A sudden image of Little Boy Blue sprang full-blown into her mind and started her giggling. "It must have been hard for you to leave behind your panpipe and your crook," she sputtered out.

He grinned. "Okay, you're entitled to a laugh." Julia wiped away the tears and tried to compose her aching facial muscles into suitable seriousness as he continued. "But I wouldn't call our farm pastoral. Just a hundred acres of moor and rock surrounded on three sides by the Irish Sea."

"It sounds very beautiful."

"It is, in its own rugged way." His grin had faded into sober introspection. "But to me it was a prison. I spent eighteen years watching the boats sail out of the harbor wishing I was on one of them."

"And finally you were." She watched the play of emotions across his face, noticing how the flickering candlelight shadowed the slight hollow of his cheeks, accentuated the clean, well-defined curve of his jaw.

"Yes, I finally got away." He stared out the window into the darkness.

"It's so ironic. You had everything I always wanted and you couldn't wait to leave it all behind." She shook her head and gazed abstractedly into the candle flame.

"What did you always want, Julia?"

She glanced up to find his eyes on her as he rubbed one lean finger thoughtfully across his smooth chin.

"I always wanted a permanent home. My dad was in the army and we traveled around a lot. But we're digressing here. We're talking about you, remember? So where did you go from Amblesey?"

"London. Where else?" He paused while the waiter deftly removed their plates. "It drew me like a magnet. I wanted to do everything, go everywhere, but London was a start. Besides, I'd sent some pictures to a magazine down there and they'd been published."

"But you must have had to leave the island to study photography?"

He leaned back and crossed his legs. "When I was sixteen, an artist came to stay down in the village for the summer. She also happened to be a very skilled photographer and I appointed myself her unofficial assistant. God knows why, but she not only tolerated me, she taught me how to take pictures. Not just the technical skills, but the *eye*, you know? The composition."

The woman must have taught him well. His pictures were good, Julia had to give him that. Her imagination conjured Martin at sixteen, fresh and eager, all long, lean limbs and enthusiasm, his persuasive ability to charm well developed already, she had no doubt. And what else had this woman taught him? The raw directness of the thought took her aback. Why should she care where he received his romantic education?

"Anyway, after she left I saved up for a really good camera and kept on teaching myself through books. Once I got to London I managed to make some useful connections, and before I knew it, I was doing fashion photography."

"Fashion?"

He smiled at her skeptical chuckle. "Believe it or not . . . Everything happened very fast. It wasn't long before I had my own studio and was making a name for myself."

"How nice for you." Was this another embellishment? Her old doubts about his stories resurfaced in a faint burst of cynicism.

"It was nice. For a while." He sat forward again to rest his elbows on the table, cradle his chin on his laced fingers, and stare moodily into the candle flame. "I got caught up in a dizzying wave of success, everything I thought London was all about. And then I got married and that was wonderful, too, at first."

Julia sat up a little straighter. "I never knew you were married."

It would take a very special woman to entice such a free spirit into marriage. She knew a moment's curiosity about this unknown female.

"For eighteen months. She was a model I met on a shoot. We were both very young and it didn't take long to realize we'd made a big mistake. We wanted different things from life and we soon discovered we weren't the people we thought we'd married. We decided to end it before it became one of those messy situations where you end up hating each other's guts. The last time I saw Susan she was happily remarried to the head of a very successful modeling agency."

At that moment the waiter placed coffee in front of Martin and a small china pot before Julia. She poured her tea as he continued.

"You see, it didn't take more than a few years in London before I started getting bored and discontented, but the money was really good and it was hard to walk away. After a while though, even the money wasn't enough to stave off that hollow feeling I got from my work. When I left Amblesey, I'd had such dreams of adventure and travel. I wanted to do much more than take pictures of clothes. So I sold the studio and took off to Patagonia."

Julia poured milk into her tea. "I don't suppose there was much call for a fashion photographer in Patagonia. So what on earth took you there?"

"An anthropological expedition. I went as their photographer. Then I wrote an article to go with the pictures and sold it to *National Geographic*. And that was how I got into journalism."

Julia couldn't help shaking her head, thinking of her own carefully planned career, the three years of college, the lowly first job on a community newspaper. And he had just fallen into it by accident and then sold his first article to *National Geographic!*

"When I was a kid, I always dreamed of being an explorer, but there isn't much money in that these days." With an engaging smile, he stirred sugar into his coffee. "So this is the next best thing. What I love about this job is the freedom to go wherever the work takes me, to see the world."

Julia sipped her tea reflectively. She had enjoyed his company more than she would have thought possible. But it left her in a very sticky situation. How would this affect their contest for the article?

If she started looking on Martin as a friend, how could she keep up her competitive edge? Her initial antagonism had faded, to be replaced by wary fascination. And she wanted to know more.

"Okay, Julia, what is it?" His voice broke into her thoughts with his usual perceptiveness.

She met his eyes squarely. "I'm going to be honest with you. I would never have thought it possible to spend an entire evening together without our usual battles erupting."

"Yes, I'm glad you made an effort to be more agreeable."

His dry amusement earned him only a jaundiced look. "Are you implying I'm usually the one at fault?"

He smiled. "Just testing. I'm glad to see you haven't mellowed too much. I rather enjoy our little skirmishes."

"Well, I'm glad you feel that way, because that's just what I want to talk to you about. Tomorrow morning, for the purposes of the competition, I'll be back to hating your guts." He gave a low whistle and rocked back on his chair as she continued. "Let's look upon this evening as Christmas in the trenches because, believe me, I want to win this more than ever, but not by default."

His eyes were bright and challenging across the flickering flame. "Sounds very interesting, but what if you lose?"

She didn't care to think about that. "As long as I know you gave it your all and treated me as a serious rival, I wouldn't feel so bad. But if I felt you patronized me and didn't even try, I'd feel cheated, even if I won."

He pondered her words for a moment, then came forward in his chair and held out his hand. "You've got a deal."

She placed her hand in his and felt his warm fingers enclosing hers.

"Now let's go to our corners and come out fighting," he continued, but as she held his hand and looked into the depths of his blue eyes, she shivered in apprehension.

Once again she remembered the feeling of his warm, fragrant skin pressed against her lips in the darkness, the thud of his rapid heartbeat matching her own, and wondered . . . what would it feel like to be held in his arms in passion?

She pushed the thoughts aside. Admitting the possibility of liking him was one thing, but anything else was out of the question.

Julia turned up the radio and sang along at the top of her voice with The Beach Boys. Yeah, she wished she could be a California girl this cold evening. Climbing the Skyway Bridge vaulting the spangled darkness of Hamilton Harbour, she had to hang on tight to the steering wheel as the icy wind off the lake buffeted her little Escort.

The closer she got to Niagara-on-the-Lake, the more she found herself wondering what Martin had been up to all day. She hadn't set eyes on him since dinner last night.

He hadn't been in the library, where she'd spent all morning going through the microfiche files. She hadn't seen him at the George either. Had he eaten breakfast at the diner? No doubt that would please Trudi. The thought brought a grin to her lips. And no doubt either that Eric would be there, keeping a strict eye on his infatuated fiancée.

Flicking on the indicator, she passed a slow-moving tractor trailer. Time to shake off that train of thought and concentrate on work. She felt so excited and focused on the story now.

How frustrating it had been this morning, not finding more information about the paywagon theft in any of the military records or old histories at either the archives or the library in Niagara. And Eric hadn't held out much hope when she told him of her plan to check the provincial archives in Toronto. He had reminded her of the discouraging possibility that the story simply wasn't true. But something was niggling away at her about this, some instinct that told her to keep on digging.

The headlights knifed through the darkness ahead of her and WELCOME TO NIAGARA-ON-THE-LAKE flashed by. Julia eased off on the gas pedal and slowed down as she drove into town.

She was glad she'd followed her hunch. What a triumphant feeling of vindication had gone through her this afternoon at the archives in Toronto when she turned up an American army document that had fallen into British hands. A document that seemed to confirm the story in the old journal.

The report told how a paywagon loaded with Spanish silver had disappeared at the Niagara frontier on the eve of the planned invasion. In between dire warnings that the unpaid militia were on the verge of desertion, it had also hinted that high-ranking officers were involved in the theft. The story reported in the old journal had implied British officers were involved, too. And suddenly she'd realized why it all sounded so familiar. High-ranking British officers, high-ranking American officers, a black marketeer, who would have been a civilian maybe. And the coins. Spanish silver, Dr. McLaughlin had said.

Julia felt the pent-up excitement building in her again even just thinking about it. Could she have hit on something even bigger than she'd first suspected? Could it be that those remains were what was left of those conspirators?

On the other hand, it could all be a colossal coincidence, and how could she ever prove it? There had been only a couple hundred coins. A paywagon would have held thousands. If those coins had come from the paywagon, where had the rest gone?

Even though she knew the chances were slim of unraveling a two-hundred-year-old mystery, still she felt elated. On a subconscious level she must have caught the similarity between the two stories and something had driven her to keep on digging. She *did* have what it took to be a good journalist. Maybe she couldn't solve the mystery, but it would add color to her article, leave the reader wondering, as she was wondering, whether the bodies were those of the conspirators.

The dashboard clock read six-fifty as Julia pulled into the tiny graveled parking lot beside the George. In the pool of yellow light cast by the brass carriage lamps on either side of the door, she saw a tall, lean figure taking the porch steps two at a time.

Her heart gave a funny little jolt and speeded up a notch. It must be relief at making it back intact through the crazy rush-hour traffic on the QEW. It couldn't have anything to do with the welcoming smile on Martin's face as he turned, came back down to her car, and opened her door.

In his jeans and parka, blond hair flopping over his

forehead, he was back to the familiar mess she knew. Yet he seemed different. Or maybe he hadn't changed at all and the difference lay in her own feelings.

"Hi there." He held out his gloved hand and she took it, allowing him to help her out of the car. "Where have you been all day?"

Oblivious to the icy buffeting wind that pulled tendrils of hair from her chignon to whip them across her freezing cheeks, Julia smiled up at him, basking in the warmth of his welcome and feeling as though she'd come home to someone who cared.

"Oh, no . . . I forgot." He struck his forehead with a gloved palm. "I'm not supposed to ask about work."

Her smile faded and she felt like an idiot. She'd been so adamant about laying down the ground rules last night. If all it took was a smile from him to send them from her head, she was in big trouble. Ducking back into the car for her purse, she took the opportunity to collect herself, acutely aware of him not a foot away behind her, stamping his feet against the cold.

"Are you trying to lull me into a false sense of security by playing fair?" She turned to face him again, hoping her voice conveyed the proper amount of irony so he wouldn't guess his disturbing effect on her.

He smiled down into her eyes with an intimacy that made her feel awkward and shy and unable to meet his gaze. She spun away and hurried up the steps onto the wooden porch.

"You're the most suspicious woman I've ever met. What can I do to make you trust me?"

Despite his plaintive tone, she didn't need to turn around to know those blue eyes were filled with mocking laughter. She gave him a sidelong look over her shoulder.

"Don't knock yourself out. I doubt very much there's anything you can do to make me trust you."

He clutched at his chest dramatically and staggered

up the steps to wrap himself drunkenly around the pillar at the top and lift soulful eyes to her. "You've wounded me to the core."

She fought down the laughter bubbling up inside and gave him a scornful look before sweeping through the door into the lobby.

He dashed ahead of her and barred her way to the stairs. "That's it. This is your last chance to be nice to me, or I won't tell you my surprise."

She bit her lip to keep from smiling at his bad imitation of Cary Grant. "Would you just remove yourself from my path? Nothing you do could possibly surprise me." Pushing past him, she started up the stairs.

"Now there's a challenge I can't resist. How about this?"

Before she knew what was happening he had spun her around, ignoring her yelp of surprise. She barely had time to register the gleam of deviltry in his eyes before his lips came down on hers in a hard, quick kiss.

SEVEN

The kiss probably lasted for only a few seconds but it felt more like hours. Then she was free and gazing into blue eyes full of mischief.

"Was that surprising enough for you?" He stood on the step below, laughing at her.

That was an understatement. If his kiss had taken her off guard, then her reaction to it had been even more unexpected. There was a dull roaring in her ears and she could feel her blood pounding crazily through her veins. She had to escape, to get away from him, before he guessed the intensity of her reaction to his little joke.

She turned on her heel and dashed up the stairs, the burning imprint of his mouth still on her lips.

His voice followed her, the laughter changing to alarm. "Julia, wait a minute. I was only . . ."

"Oh, there you are, Martin . . ."

With a groan of frustration, he gripped the banister and turned at the sound of Amy's voice in the hallway below.

Oh God, not now! Torn with indecision, he paused with one foot on the next step, wanting desperately to run after her. A door slammed somewhere above. What had he done?

Amy came to the foot of the stairs with a sheaf of yellow papers in her hand. "My, but you're popular. All sorts of people trying to get hold of you . . ."

He paid no attention to her careful recitation of his phone messages. His mind was still reeling from the electricity that had shot through his body at the touch of her lips on his and the sick sensation in the pit of his stomach when she reacted to his kiss with such anger. He felt like a first-class jackass. How could he have been so stupid?

Julia leaned back against the door and pressed her hands to her flaming cheeks. She couldn't contain the overwhelming reaction for even ten more seconds. Taking slow, deep breaths, she struggled to get her racing heartbeat under control. What had happened to her?

Now that she'd become aware of him, it seemed to be snowballing. This was awful—that just a peck on the lips could affect her like this. She lunged away from the door and began pacing the small space between the foot of the bed and the window like a trapped animal.

She paused at the dresser to flick on the lamp, and a strange face stared back from the large oval mirror. Was that wild-looking creature really her? Bright red splotches blazed on her cheeks, contrasting vividly with her pale skin. Whipped by the wind, strands of her auburn hair stood on end like a garden rake. Looking like this, she could frighten small children. But what scared her most was the hunted look in her wide violet eyes. There was no way she could face Martin without his guessing the turmoil of her emotions.

With unsteady hands she pulled out the pins from her hair and shook it loose, then picked up the brush from the dresser and attacked the thick wavy strands with vigorous strokes. Even Amy wouldn't keep him forever. He'd be up any minute and she couldn't let him see her like this. She'd better get herself under control.

With deft fingers she laced her hair into a French braid. As she twisted on the elastic to hold it in place, she paused as a more disturbing thought struck her. What if he'd really kissed her? Taken her in his arms and slowly and thoroughly kissed her into mindless ecstasy. She swallowed hard and licked her suddenly dry lips. At the rate she was going that would take about two seconds.

Finishing her hair, she stepped over to the window. In the glow of the street lamp on the corner she could see a few fat flakes of snow drifting down. It had been much easier before, when her feelings toward him hadn't been so ambivalent.

Wait a minute. She spun away from the window. What had happened here? How did she get from admitting to herself last night that she felt physically attracted to him to thinking in terms of *feelings* today?

A knock on the door made her hold her breath and freeze in place.

"Julia . . . Please open the door. I'm sorry, my dear. I never meant to offend you. I was just teasing."

She slowly let out her breath in relief and smiled. He thought she was angry! It was a darned sight better than his thinking she was one of those witless women who went brain dead at the touch of a man's lips on hers. *Yeah, you can joke about it now, but you didn't think it was so funny five minutes ago.*

The knock sounded again. "I don't blame you for being angry. That was a stupid, childish stunt to pull. Please realize I didn't mean any harm. We made such progress last night. I thought we were starting to become friends. If I've done anything to jeopardize that . . ." His voice trailed off helplessly.

She tiptoed over to the door and pressed her ear up against it. He thought they were starting to become friends. She felt a warm glow settle on her and smiled, hugging herself with the strangest, sweetest feeling of happiness.

"Julia? . . ." His voice turned low and coaxing.

What was she going to do? She could go on letting him think she was angry, but that would be dishonest. On the other hand, she couldn't let him see how disturbing that kiss had been. And she couldn't stay in here forever. Suddenly an impish smile curved her lips. She moved back and whipped open the door. Martin flinched, his eyes widening in surprise as she stepped toward him, scowling.

She couldn't maintain the expression more than ten seconds. Then the grin she had been fighting broke out unrestrained.

"Had you worried, didn't I?" She wagged her finger in his face.

For a moment he stared dumbfounded. Then realization dawned in his eyes and he threw back his head and laughed. "God, you had me scared. I thought you were about to dispatch me to join the captain in his celestial haunting ground."

"And you would have deserved it." Infected by his laughter, Julia leaned against her doorjamb for support. "You should have seen your face!" she crowed.

"You should have seen yours." He leaned back against his door, shaking with helpless laughter.

Julia wiped at the tears, unable to bring her giggling under control. Partly it was pure relief at scraping through the situation with her pride intact. If he ever found out how she had really been affected by that kiss, she'd never be able to face him again.

"I've got to hand it to you, my dear girl, you've got depths of silliness I would never have expected." He composed his face and straightened up, but a smile full of warmth and intimacy lit his eyes as he came toward her.

"Yeah, well keep it under your hat, I've got a reputation to protect." Once again Julia felt lightheaded with happiness. It was crazy that a shared moment of idiocy should make her feel this way.

He placed one hand on the lintel above her head and leaned slightly toward her. "So do you still want to know what my surprise is?" His husky voice held a teasing, provocative note that made her breath catch in her throat for a moment.

"Yes, with one stipulation." She put a warning hand against his chest, feeling his slow, steady heartbeat beneath the cream wool of his Aran sweater. Her traitorous fingers wanted to linger and explore the enticing contours of firm muscle under her palm. Snatching her hand away, she shoved it resolutely behind her back.

"No more kisses," she croaked, then cleared her throat. She couldn't be responsible for her actions a second time around.

He chuckled, low and husky. "How unflattering to my male ego. All right, I promise, no more kisses. Now grab your purse, we're going out. And don't ask me where." He tugged her hand.

"Wait a minute." She yanked it away and stepped back, remembering her fashion lapse the night before. "Am I appropriately dressed?"

He paused in the doorway, looking at her over his shoulder, then turned and moved toward her. With a disconcerting smile in his eyes, he reached for the top button of her coat. Slipping it open, his hand slid down to the next until, with exquisite deliberation, he had unfastened them all, one button at a time. Julia stood rooted to the spot, unable to breath.

As he slowly parted the coat, his eyes locked with hers, a sultry, tantalizing quality in the darkening blue depths. Why couldn't she breathe? Why couldn't she move? If she were lucky, maybe she could slip quietly and unobtrusively into a coma.

His gaze dropped to her running shoes, then began a slow, appraising ascent up her denim-clad legs, lingering on the curve of her slim hips. Why hadn't she thrown these old jeans out? They were far too snug and left nothing to his imagination, she could tell by the imperceptible widening of his narrowed eyes before they continued their exploration. Over the soft blue muslin shirt, lingering on the swell of her breasts exposed by her open neckline. That top button had come undone again, she just knew it without even looking down. The hot flush she felt traveling up her body with his caressing gaze now flamed into her face.

"You'll do." He met her eyes and Julia didn't want to think about what he saw there. But his expression suddenly became serious, and he turned away and stepped out into the hall.

Julia fastened her coat with fingers that trembled slightly, picked up her purse, and followed him out, shutting the door quietly behind her. Her heart was beating a mile a minute and her knees felt weak and unsteady. What had just happened?

She had felt his leisured appraisal as if he were running his hands over her body, as if he were making love to her . . . and he hadn't even touched her.

But how had it affected him? How she wished she could read him as easily as he could read her.

Catching up with him at the top of the stairs, she forced herself to respond in kind to the teasing grin he turned on her. Once again they were back in familiar territory and that odd little moment might never have happened. Perhaps it never did, except in her overheated imagination.

Whatever the case, this was much safer, she told herself, as she walked ahead of him down the stairs and out into the cold, starry night.

* * *

"Of course you know what Oscar Wilde said about Niagara Falls, don't you?" Martin leaned his elbows on the icy railing and looked out on the spectacular, thundering torrent, the plume of spray illuminated by multicolored floodlights.

Julia smiled and shook her head. "No, but I'm sure you're going to tell me."

He gave her a sideways look, a telltale quirk at the corner of his mouth. "He claimed it was the second biggest disappointment of marriage."

"And do you agree with him?" she asked lightly.

"No, I think they're quite overwhelming . . . and very beautiful."

"That's not what I meant. Do you share his disparaging views on marriage?"

Julia turned to study the wooded hillside across the road, unable for some reason to meet his eyes. Without even looking, she was acutely aware that they held a gleam of speculation as he stared at her.

The spray from the falls had frozen on the trees, turning them into glittering, icy jewels. With big, thick flakes of snow drifting down from the sky, it looked like a winter fairyland. She waited, surprised by her own anxiety to know his answer and appalled to think that once again he would see right through her.

After an interminable pause he said, "My own brief experience of marriage hardly qualifies me to judge." He sounded calm and matter-of-fact. "Unlike Wilde, I wouldn't make a sweeping condemnation. It's not something I've given much thought to doing again, but I'm sure it's right for some people."

She turned back to him and caught his smile, returning it mechanically. Well, that was that. Whatever made her ask that question anyway? What did it matter?

"So if you're concerned about some poor unsuspecting female being hog-tied to a pompous windbag like me, you can put your fears to rest."

Her laughter sounded hollow to her own ears. "That's a great weight off my mind, thank you."

He took her elbow and they began walking along the footpath toward the parking lot where Martin had left the battered old Honda.

He had surprised her, as promised, with a trip to Niagara Falls for dinner. And once again she had spent a completely agreeable evening in his company. Until recently she'd failed to appreciate his sense of humor, but tonight she found him witty and fascinating.

When he regaled her with more of his exploits, she'd had no trouble believing them this time, or allowing herself to be charmed and entertained by him. And she found herself telling him of her own travels.

Martin had listened attentively as she recounted her father's experiences at the Canadian Embassy in Iran during the revolt against the Shah and laughed out loud at some of her more reckless exploits at English boarding school.

Getting into the car for the short drive back to the George, Julia felt sorry the evening was over. She buckled her seatbelt in the close confines of the Honda, acutely conscious of the powerful attraction this man held for her. He possessed a force of character so strong it stamped itself on everything he touched. Even his rented wreck had become an extension of his roguish personality. Was this happening to her, too?

He drove with the same smooth physical assurance that marked all his other actions, she noticed, as they followed the Niagara Parkway that hugged the river's edge. As he slowed down for the turn as they reached the town, Julia found her gaze drawn irresistibly by the taut thigh muscles flexing beneath the blue denim as he hit the clutch, by his lean, strong hand on the gearshift lever between them.

All evening as she sat across the small table for two she had tingled with simmering awareness. The shyness she felt when his eyes smiled into hers, the little buzz that went racing through her with every accidental touch, all these things only seemed to be affecting her. Martin treated her with friendly neutrality. If he felt anything else, he kept it well hidden.

His soft voice broke into her thoughts. "You're very quiet. I hope you enjoyed the evening."

Had she really enjoyed the evening? From the moment she arrived at the inn tonight she'd run the gamut of emotions. *Enjoyment* seemed much too insipid a word to describe the way he made her feel.

"Yes, I enjoyed myself. But I have to admit that if we spend too many more evenings this amicably I'm going to find you a deadly bore."

He laughed. "I wouldn't get too worried if I were you. I'm sure to do something before too long to put your nose out of joint. I seem to have a propensity for causing trouble, wouldn't you say?"

"I'll agree to that." Julia was thankful he couldn't possibly interpret her fervent response. He'd caused her emotions more trouble than any other man she'd ever met. There, she'd finally admitted it to herself.

Back at the inn, standing in the hallway outside their doors, Julia lingered awkwardly. "Well . . . um . . . thank you. I really did have a nice evening."

He stood with his hands shoved in the pockets of his jeans, smiling at her. "I had a nice time, too. I'll see you in the morning. Guess you'll be back to hating my guts again, right?"

She pushed her door open behind her and laughed. "I've really got you running scared, haven't I?"

But the smile was slowly fading from his face as he stared beyond her into her room with a look of growing shock. Slowly she turned around, following the direction of his gaze and gasped.

"Oh, my God!"

Her room looked as though it had been torn apart by an enraged animal. Every drawer had been pulled out and the contents dumped on the floor. The closet doors stood open and the clothes that had hung there lay strewn across the bed, which had been stripped right down to the mattress. The pile of papers she had left on the bedside table lay crumpled and scattered around the room.

She slowly walked in, dimly aware that Martin had followed her, his hand on her shoulder. He left for a second, then returned. "My room hasn't been touched."

Julia walked dazedly around the room, trying to see what was missing. "I can't believe this. Please tell me I'm dreaming."

Her voice thickened and trembled. She felt on the brink of tears, beset by the awful, vulnerable feeling that someone could violate her life like this.

Martin took her by the shoulders, pulled her close to him, and put his arms around her. "Now calm down, Julia. Is anything missing?"

"I . . . I don't know. It's hard to tell in this mess." She tried to control her shaking voice, drawing comfort from the solid warmth of his body against hers, the slight rasp of his chin against her temple.

He gazed down at her, intent. "Look, if you can cope for a few minutes, I'm going to tell Amy. Don't touch anything yet."

After Martin went downstairs, Julia pulled off her coat and walked around the room again, making a mental inventory. Nothing seemed to be missing. Pausing by the dresser, she gave a little cry of relief and picked up the delicately worked gold bracelet her parents had given her on graduating from college.

Why hadn't the thieves made off with that? It didn't make sense. But perhaps they were only interested in money and she'd had her purse with her. Julia slumped down onto the bed, feeling sick. Someone had been in her room, handling her things. The thought made her flesh crawl. Then suddenly she realized her briefcase was nowhere to be seen.

A minute later Martin returned, preceded by an out-of-breath Amy in a pale blue chenille robe and hairnet.

"My poor child!" Shock and concern creased her motherly face as she gazed openmouthed around the ransacked room.

With a small cry Julia rushed into Martin's arms and they closed around her. "They've got my briefcase. All the notes I took today are in there. I'll have to do the work all over again and . . ." She knew she was babbling, but somehow couldn't help herself. ". . . I've got my expense credit cards in there, the access codes to the office . . ." Her words became increasingly wobbly and tremulous, her fingers plucked at the soft wool of his sweater in agitation as tears began to roll down her cheeks.

"Wait a minute, wait a minute." His arms tightened around her. "You had your briefcase with you today? In your car?" She sniffed and nodded against his shoulder. "I didn't see you bring it in this evening."

She pulled away and looked up at him through the tears, wiping impatiently at her eyes. "You're right! I left it behind the seat."

"Give me your keys. I'll check your car to make sure." He was already heading out the door.

"You poor thing." Amy, who had been wringing her hands and exclaiming in agitation over the state of the room, bustled over to Julia and patted her shoulder. "This is just awful. Nothing like this has ever happened before . . . I mean, at this time of year it's just unheard of . . ." she rambled on in broken sentences. "But is anything gone? Of course we'll replace anything you've lost."

Julia shook her head dazedly and turned as Martin came back through the door.

"Your case is safe and sound. I locked it in your trunk."

"Well, that's something anyway," the landlady sighed. "I know, I'll make you a nice cup of tea. My mother always said hot, sweet tea was the best thing for shock." And she swept back out of the room, happy to have something to do.

Martin held out his hand, and Julia stared at it without comprehension, then up to meet the compassionate look in his eyes. "Come on, old girl. Let's go and have that cup of tea, shall we?" Putting her hand in his, she let him pull her to her feet. "The police are on their way."

It was twelve-thirty by the time the gangly young police officer had departed, Martin had dispatched a tired, upset Amy off to bed, and Julia trekked back upstairs to face the daunting prospect of putting her room back in order again. She stood in the doorway, hardly knowing where to start. As nothing had been stolen, the officer told her the thief had probably been interrupted in his search for money.

"It's a mess, but between the two of us it shouldn't take long." At the sound of his voice she turned to see Martin standing close behind her. "I'll give you a hand." Moving past her, he began picking up the drawers and putting them back in place.

His quick, energetic movements helped her focus on what had to be done, and she made a start hanging clothes back in the wardrobe and picking up the papers strewn around the room.

A low whistle sounded behind her and she looked over to see Martin standing by the dresser, holding up her black silk and lace teddy. With a small, speculative smile curving the corners of his mouth, his knowing gaze went from the flimsy piece of silk to her and back again, as if he were imagining how it would look on her and enjoying the view.

Julia strode over and snatched it from his fingers. With one hand on his chest, she started pushing him backward toward the door. "Thank you for all your help, now good night!"

One final push sent him out into the hallway, where he bowed low with a mocking flourish. "Good night. Enemy mine."

She closed the door on his smiling face and turned to lean against the wood panel, teddy still clutched to her chest, a slow grin forming on her lips. He had been so sweet and helpful, taking charge with an air of quiet strength, not the blustering bravado she might once have expected. When he held her in his arms, she had felt safe and protected, as if she could depend on him.

Good grief, what was she thinking! Depend on Martin Taylor? What a joke. She could never, *ever* depend on him. By his own admission he wanted no ties, no responsibilities to hold him back when he was ready to move on. He was a casual friend. Nothing more.

Her gaze fell to the silky teddy in her hands and she thought of the look in his eyes when he unbuttoned her coat. It made her feel warm and shivery just thinking about it. *Come on, Julia. A friend?* Was that how she honestly thought of him?

Sunday evenings were busy at the diner. The red vinyl booths were crowded with older couples out for the evening and young families taking a break from domestic routine.

Julia sat in her corner booth waiting patiently for a menu. Trudi and the other waitress had their hands full and she didn't mind waiting. She'd been working all day and there was nothing to do now that everything was closed and nothing ahead of her but a long, dull Sunday evening.

"Mind if I join you?"

Julia looked up to see Eric Galway's round, freckled face and shook her head. "Not at all."

She smiled at him, happy to have some company. Besides, she wanted to tell him about her discovery in the Toronto archives. He might be interested now.

He slid into the opposite seat, slipped off his heavy tweed coat, and rubbed his hands together. "So, how's the research going?"

"Not bad. My trip to Toronto wasn't a complete waste of time after all." She leaned closer to him. "Remember that old journal entry about the paywagon robbery? At least I know now that story wasn't a myth."

He raised wiry red eyebrows. "Oh really? How fascinating." His tone of voice told her that he didn't find it fascinating at all. She got the distinct impression he wasn't in a good mood. "But surely there are incidents of greater historical importance that would be better documented."

Julia felt slightly let down. Eric obviously thought it a pretty frivolous episode to waste her time on, or maybe he just wasn't in the mood for talking about it.

After studying his menu for a minute, he waved impatiently to Trudi a few tables away. Julia could have sworn the other woman noticed Eric's gesture, but she seemed to deliberately turn her back on him. Trudi gave the empty table another wipe and carefully tidied the condiments.

No wonder Eric was in a bad mood. It didn't take Sigmund Freud to see that he and Trudi must have had an argument. He sat drumming his fingers impatiently on the brown countertop, clearly itching to say or do something.

When Trudi came over a minute later to take their orders, she didn't even look at her fiancé but gave Julia a bright smile.

"Hi, Julia, how're you doing this evening . . . and where's that handsome friend of yours been hiding?" She might be acting as if Eric were invisible, but her words were clearly intended for him.

"He went back to Toronto for the weekend," Julia murmured quickly.

Each second that went by her discomfort increased. She wished wholeheartedly that Eric had sat elsewhere. Surely Trudi couldn't fail to see the icy look in her fiancé's eyes, but she still went on.

"Oh, if he were my boyfriend, I wouldn't let him out of my sight for a second."

Julia cringed inside. The comment was so obviously designed to annoy Eric, she wanted to slink down under the table and vanish. Eric saved her from responding.

"If you're done with your gossiping, would you mind taking our orders?"

Trudi didn't even acknowledge his tart, edgy words except to fix her gaze on Julia and smile even more brightly. "So what'll it be tonight, Julia?"

She asked for fish and chips and Eric added his order. Trudi took it down without even casting a glance his way. With another warm smile at Julia, she dashed away to the next table, where a toddler had just spilled his milk and was setting up a wail.

How she hated being caught in the middle of this. They had obviously been arguing over Trudi's flirtation with Martin and it was all so silly. He wasn't worth arguing over. After all, he wasn't seriously interested and he'd soon be gone.

But still, she could readily understand how Eric might feel threatened by Martin's aura of success and self-confidence. How many times had she envied his easy self-assurance in any situation? How many times had she felt insecure and unsure of herself and tried to cover up? She could really feel for Eric. It must be hard to live with. And hard to lie to yourself.

Turning her gaze out the window again, Julia saw Martin coming down the sidewalk. He met her eyes and smiled, and at six o'clock on a dark, cold winter's evening she felt a warm glow spreading inside her, as if the summer sun had just come out.

He had left on Saturday morning, whether to pursue his research or for personal reasons, she didn't know. But she had to admit one thing. She had missed him. And now he had returned.

She darted a quick glance at Eric. He had seen Martin, too. His face had become even more rigid in his anger. This was the worst possible thing that could have happened. In this volatile situation Martin's presence could be the match to the fuse.

She heard the door open behind her and felt her heart pounding uncomfortably in her chest. Then he was standing beside the table, looking down at her with that small, intimate smile that did strange things to her pulse rate. For a moment nothing else mattered.

"Hi." The single word sounded like a caress.

"Nice to see you back." Did that sound too eager? Was her voice too husky? She didn't mean to sound provocative.

His eyes slid over to Eric and he nodded a greeting. Eric returned it with icy restraint. With a look Julia wanted to think was regret, Martin passed on to the next booth and slid into the seat facing her.

Trudi appeared at his side in scant seconds with a menu and a dazzling smile. "I like the new look, Martin."

She leaned forward to stroke a caressing finger across his clean-shaven jaw, and he shot her a heart-stopping grin full of boyish recklessness.

From that moment on Julia was just waiting for Eric to explode. His mouth set in a grim line as he stared unseeingly at the paper placemat advertising the weekly specials, his attention clearly riveted on the conversation behind him.

". . . and remember that friend of my grandmother's I told you about?" Trudi burbled on enthusiastically. "The one who knows everything that ever happened around here since the year zero. She just got back from Miami with her daughter and I can take you to meet her if you like."

"Oh, Trudi, you are a love," Martin responded. "That would be wonderful. Ring me at the George and we'll set something up."

The bell sounded and Trudi floated back to the kitchen with a euphoric smile on her face.

Julia felt a little irked. Couldn't he tone down the charm a bit? If he carried on this way, poor Eric might have a fit. Worse yet, Trudi might take him seriously. And judging by the speed with which the waitress dumped their orders in front of them and returned to Martin's booth, that might very well be the case.

"So . . ." Trudi breathed, "you never did finish telling me that story the other day. The one about the time you spent with the pygmies in the Congo and had to eat an elephant."

"Not the whole elephant, love. Just a few choice fillets." The impish wink he turned in Julia's direction told her he was including her in the joke.

But she looked down at her plate, in no mood to be amused and starting to become really annoyed. Did he have to entertain himself by turning his charm on every woman he met? She'd already told him what trouble he inadvertently caused last time. What was his game now? Especially with Eric sitting right there. It must be obvious even to Martin that the other man was fit to be tied. Was he doing it just to make mischief?

Trudi leaned on the back of his booth, gazing at Martin with a dreamy expression. "You've had such an exciting life, done so many exciting things, been to so many fascinating places.'' She raised her voice slightly. ''Unlike *some* people I know.''

Julia winced inside. Poor Eric.

''Well then, Trudi my dear, you're definitely hanging with the wrong crowd.'' Martin smiled as Trudi reluctantly obeyed the insistent ringing of the bell and returned to the kitchen for her next order.

Julia stared down at her plate, but her fish and chips had lost their appeal and she noticed that Eric hadn't even touched his steak. Angry color flooded his face, and he sat with his head half turned away. How could Martin be so insensitive?

Trudi returned with his meal and lingered by the booth to talk as Martin took a bite of his cheeseburger. ''Ooh . . . you have a little scar right here.''

Right where? Julia dropped her fork with a clatter and her head jerked upright. Eric had now turned fully around in his seat and the back of his neck glowed beet red.

''How far down does it go?'' Trudi's wandering fingers were now probing beneath the collar of Martin's white cotton shirt. With a sheepish grin at Julia that she didn't return, he detached Trudi's fingers from his neck and applied himself studiously to his burger once more.

Sure. Play innocent. As if he didn't like stirring up trouble. She felt a sick churning in her stomach and pushed her plate away.

Trudi turned a dismissive glance on Eric's anger that Julia could have sworn held a tinge of triumph and sashayed off into the kitchen. Mouth set in a furious line, he threw his napkin down on the table and followed her.

Julia slipped her arms into her coat, snatched up her purse, and slid out of the booth. Determined not to look in Martin's direction, she left the money for her bill on the table. She couldn't sit there a moment longer. Without a backward glance, she rushed out, almost glad to feel the cold wind whipping her heated face.

She hadn't gone half a block before she heard him calling out and the sound of running footsteps behind her.

"Julia, wait." He caught up with her, breathing hard from the exertion, his breath pluming in the cold air. "What's your hurry?"

"It's too cold for a stroll." She lengthened her stride, not wanting to look at him, but he kept up beside her effortlessly.

"I wasn't talking about that. You left without finishing your dinner."

"I wasn't hungry anymore," she bit off, panting slightly as she increased her pace in the effort to shake him off.

"Why are you angry with me, Julia?" His voice was quiet. He didn't sound as if he was having any trouble keeping up.

"I'm not angry with you." Her voice rose. "What makes you think I'm angry with you?"

Suddenly he clamped her upper arm with a strong grip, forcing her to stop her headlong flight and spinning her around to face his questioning eyes.

"Okay, so you're not angry. So why did you just flounce out of the restaurant like a kid having a temper tantrum?"

"I didn't flounce. I left." She wrenched her arm out of his grasp and strode away, hardly aware of the icy wind hitting her full in the face as she turned the corner onto King Street. She had no right to be angry with him. After all, it had nothing to do with her. Trudi was a grown woman who could look out for herself.

"If you must know, I couldn't stomach another minute of that nauseating display." The words tumbled out, despite her intention to say nothing.

He caught up with her again. ''What are you talking about?''

''Do you have to flirt with every woman within your orbit? Has it never occurred to you that Trudi could take you seriously and get hurt?''

''Just hold on a minute. I was not flirting with her.''

Now she could hear anger hardening his voice, and somehow it gave her a perverse satisfaction.

''If anything, she was flirting with me,'' he said impatiently.

''I didn't see you fighting her off with a stick!''

''What could I do? Be rude to the poor girl? I couldn't be so thoughtlessly cruel.''

''Oh really?'' She stopped abruptly and her laughter held only cold sarcasm. ''When did you change? You were never that scrupulous in the past.''

He ran a hand through his hair in frustration. ''What the hell are we talking about now?''

''Never mind.'' She glared up at him. He had such a convenient memory, but she hadn't forgotten all those slighting comments and cruel digs he'd made at her expense. ''You men are all the same.''

She turned and dashed down the dark street, past the last block of small clapboard houses toward the lights of the George.

''Now there's an intelligent answer. Well, you know what I think, Julia?'' he called out after her.

''No, and I don't care.''

Her footsteps crunched loudly as she dashed across the gravel parking lot and ran up the steps to the porch, hearing him close behind.

''I think you're acting like a jealous woman.''

His quiet, measured words hit her like a sledgehammer. With a hand on the doorknob, she turned to see him standing at the bottom of the steps. The anger had vanished from his face and he gazed up at her with a thoughtful expression.

A cold shiver went through her. "Well, if that isn't the height of conceit. Me? Jealous?"

Her scornful face made Martin suddenly feel incredibly foolish. God, that was a presumptuous thing to have said. Her opinion of him was low enough as it was, and no matter what he did, he seemed fated to keep adding to her already lengthy list of unflattering labels for him. Now she could add *narcissistic* to the catalog.

But a second ago he'd been so sure. And there'd been so many times when his life had depended on his ability to read people. Whether the sweaty kid with the frightened eyes would really pull that trigger. Whether the harmless-looking old man was a simple peasant or a hardened party member ready to turn him in.

Well, whether he was right or not this time, it was bloody arrogant of him to have come out and said it. He owed her an apology.

Martin suddenly bounded up the steps toward her, and Julia threw open the door in panic, just about falling into the warm, brightly lit lobby of the George with him hard on her heels.

"I don't give a damn what you do or who you do it with!" she yelled over her shoulder. "Just stay away from me!"

"Did you have a nice evening, my dears?"

Julia stopped dead at the sight of Amy's smiling face. No, she couldn't stand making small talk right now. Her whole body was trembling with the sickening realization that Martin had hit the nail on the head. And he knew it.

EIGHT

Another plate heaped with fish and chips slid slowly past her on the white arborite counter. Julia reached out to grab it, but she couldn't seem to move fast enough and could only watch with horrified eyes as it slid off the end and crashed onto the floor. Down at the other end of the long counter, wearing skimpy black lace underwear, Trudi leaned over to smile provocatively into Martin's appreciative blue eyes.

Julia could feel her heart thudding painfully against her ribs as she struggled to waken. She took a deep breath, desperate to fill her lungs with air and fight off the cloying sense of utter insignificance. They'd been so fascinated by each other she could have dropped dead and neither of them would have noticed. It had only been a dream. But that didn't dispel the sick, empty feeling inside her.

For a moment she felt completely disoriented, until she shivered and turned over, huddling smaller under her quilt. Through the window, beyond the bare trees, she could see a few stars sprinkling the night-dark sky.

In drowsy fascination, she watched the graceful movement of the long lace curtains, billowing gently in the breeze. They could be the pale, flowing skirts of a ghostly maiden, she thought, keeping a nightly vigil for her lover lost across the water.

Suddenly her eyes snapped wide and every muscle in her body clenched into alertness. The window stood open by a foot.

She held her breath, straining to identify a faint noise somewhere in the dense silence, in the darkness. It was the sound of ragged breathing. She was not alone.

The knowledge almost sent her pounding heart leaping from her chest, but Julia forced herself to stay still. Please God, let this be a nightmare. The idea of women being raped in their homes or hotel rooms was something she thought she'd left behind in Toronto.

Don't panic. Think. Logically assess the situation. As long as the intruder believed she was still asleep, it gave her a few seconds' grace. Without moving so much as a fraction, she swept frantic eyes around the area near her bed, looking for anything that could serve as a weapon. The small travel alarm on the bedside table was the only object of any weight she could see, and that wouldn't do any damage.

All at once a giddy feeling of relief swept over her. Martin lay sleeping just across the hall. If he'd wakened the other night at the sound of her stumbling around downstairs, then surely she could rouse him with a good yell. And maybe the noise alone would be enough to scare the man off. *Martin.* She clung to the thought of his strength and dependability like a drowning woman to a lifeline.

Her heightened senses caught a stealthy footfall near the bottom of the bed. Oh God, he was coming for her. She felt a sudden stab of intense fear. What if he was armed? But there was nothing for it. She had to do it now. She took a deep breath. Okay . . . one, two, three.

A figure moved into her field of vision. The faint

light from the window picked out the sheen of brass buttons and tarnished gold braid, the dull glow of a short scarlet jacket.

She jolted upright with Martin's name tearing from her throat in a scream that was no longer a calculated response but primitive, unreasoning terror. The shadowy figure by the wardrobe gasped and started back. Then she heard a loud thud. The intruder lunged for the window, threw up the sash, and disappeared into the night.

A second later her door burst open.

"Julia?"

She sagged in relief at the reassuring strength in Martin's urgent voice. It had to be the most welcome sound she'd ever heard.

"He went out the window," she gasped, her voice shaking along with the rest of her body. Martin didn't wait to hear any more. He followed in the intruder's footsteps out onto the upstairs veranda.

Julia sat huddled in her bed, the covers drawn up tightly to her chin, shivering more from residual fear than the icy breeze. She didn't dare turn on the bedside lamp. Even through the darkness she could tell Martin hadn't wasted time dressing. As he climbed out the window, she had caught a glimpse of the tight, smooth curve of his buttocks.

A moment later he climbed back in, panting slightly in the dark, and closed the sash. "I'm sorry, he got away. Now, Julia, are you all right?"

Silhouetted against the pale rectangle of the window, she could see the soft gleam of bare flesh outlining his broad shoulders and narrow hips as he approached the bed.

"I'm fine," she answered in a small voice. All she wanted was to launch herself into the security of his arms, but she didn't dare.

"Hang on for a minute, I'll be right back." He was already through the door.

Scrambling out of bed, she turned on the lamp, blinking against the unaccustomed brightness and shivering in the chill air.

A moment later he returned wearing a short, faded blue velour bathrobe and immediately put his arms around her, drawing her close to his warmth.

"It's all right, love, calm down. You're safe."

But she couldn't control the trembling and let him press her head against his shoulder. She closed her eyes for a moment, nestling her cheek against the soft velour lapel and inhaling the clean, soapy fragrance of his skin. Slowly the terror ebbed and she began to feel safe in his arms.

She allowed herself the luxury of relaxing against him while he ran his hands up and down her back, as if comforting a child. But the feel of his gentle touch on her skin through the soft flannel had begun to send ripples of pleasure through her. She had to fight the overpowering urge to wrap her arms around him and mold herself to his lean, muscled body. Julia began trembling again, this time with the intensity of her physical need for him.

"You're cold! Here, get under the covers."

He drew back, then held open the bed covers, and she scrambled in, grateful he had misinterpreted her reaction. He sat down beside her, tucking the quilt around her as if she were five years old.

"Now, what happened? Did you get a good look?"

Sitting propped against the pillows, Julia hugged herself and rubbed her arms, finding it hard to meet his eyes. "There was someone in my room. When I screamed, I guess I startled it."

"It?"

"Did I say *it?* I meant him . . . I mean . . . I don't know what I mean." She still avoided Martin's eyes.

"Julia, what are you talking about? Exactly what did you see?"

She took a deep breath. He'd never believe it. She didn't believe it herself. "I think I saw Captain Fairfax."

He stared at her for a moment. "You what?"

"I saw someone dressed in the kind of uniform officers wore in the War of 1812."

"Are you trying to tell me you saw a ghost?"

"I don't know what I saw. I only know that it was here and when I screamed it jumped out of the window."

"Bloody odd behavior for a ghost if you ask me."

Martin rose to his feet and examined the window, then slowly walked around the room. She watched as he carefully scanned the dresser and the wardrobe. Nothing seemed missing or out of place.

She found herself noticing his bare, tanned calves, the fluid, athletic grace of his lean body beneath the robe. He had the coiled, alert quality of a sleek, beautiful animal, muscles and sinews poised to respond exactly as he wished.

Martin stopped at the foot of the bed. At his feet lay a black leather briefcase, its contents strewn haphazardly over the wide pine floorboards.

"Hello, what's this?" He crouched and shoved the papers back into the case. "Did you leave this on the floor with your notes spilled all around?"

"Of course not!" The bedsprings squeaked and Julia's face appeared over the carved footboard.

"Then it looks like this is what your ghost was after." Rising to his feet, he handed her the briefcase as she knelt up on the bed.

"My briefcase?"

The covers dropped away from her demure flannel nightgown as Julia took the heavy case from his hand. The row of tiny buttons down the front stood open, revealing the creamy swell of her breasts. He couldn't let himself get sidetracked like this. He forced his gaze away from the shadowy curves and back to her face as she continued. "That must have been the thump I heard when I screamed."

"Quite possibly. And I think we can dispense with the ghost theory. After all, why would he hop out the window when he could just ooze through the wall?"

Julia gave an embarrassed nod.

"But I have to wonder, why would someone be interested in your briefcase?" Martin folded his arms and frowned. He smelled a rat. Something was all wrong about this and he didn't like it.

"I have no idea. There's nothing in here anyone would be interested in." She bent her tousled auburn head and leafed through the case. Seemingly satisfied her material was all there, she zipped the case closed and sank back on her heels.

"You know, Julia, something very strange is going on around here." He sat down on the bed again, resting his elbows on the top of the case sitting on the bed between them, and leaned toward her. "First your room is broken into, but nothing is stolen. And now this."

Her violet eyes were wide and still smoky with sleep. He could smell the warm, baby-powder scent rising from her skin under that prissy flannel nightgown and thought of the steamy bathroom that morning. Breathing in the lingering, intimate fragrance, he had found it wickedly exciting to think of the ice maiden stepping out of the shower only minutes before, warm, wet, and naked.

Someone should give him a good swift kick. What was he doing indulging in erotic fantasies at a time like this? He was responsible for her safety. And what the hell would he say to Roger if anything happened to her?

He stroked his stubble thoughtfully. "Your case was

in the car before. Maybe the reason they didn't take anything was because they didn't find what they were looking for."

"Wait a minute. Are you trying to suggest that the same person was here both times?" She stared at him as if he had lost his mind and then laughed. "That's ridiculous. What would anyone want with my briefcase?"

He felt a surge of anger. Dammit, he was trying to help her and all she could do was laugh at him. "Have you got a better explanation? Look, Julia, you said yourself that nothing was missing, in spite of the fact that you'd left jewelry on the dresser."

"So? That just means the thief was more interested in money and credit cards."

"Money I can see, but credit cards?" He shook his head. "Besides, why would he suspect you carried anything of value in your briefcase? No, I think there's something more to this."

Julia dropped the briefcase back on the floor by the night table, sat back, and folded her arms across her chest. "Okay, Sherlock, like what?"

"I don't know." He already knew the answer to his next question, but he'd ask it anyway. "What are you working on, Julia?"

She laughed. "Oh come on . . . you can't be serious."

He watched her steadily, allowing his gaze to wander from the fading merriment in her eyes to her full, soft lips where the smile slowly quivered and died.

"You *are* serious!" Julia caught her bottom lip between her teeth.

All at once it became vitally important to know what it would feel like to sink his teeth oh so gently into that luscious lower lip.

Dammit, Martin, are you crazy? If his instincts were right, and they were very seldom wrong, something was up. He needed to keep his wits about him and his libido in check. Besides, when would he ever get it through his head? The woman wasn't interested.

"Okay, okay, you caught me." Her dry voice wrenched his mind back to the subject at hand. "I've discovered the worldwide headquarters of a dangerous fascist group right here in town. I'm calling my article Nazis-by-the-Lake. Little known to anybody, they were very active during the War of 1812."

"When you're quite finished . . ." He pressed his lips together in impatience. "Someone is interested enough in something you've uncovered to risk coming to your room twice to find it."

"The only person I can think of who'd be interested in any of that information would be you." The look she slanted him had suspicion written all over it.

That was gratitude for you. "Very funny. Full of jokes tonight, aren't we? Fortunately for me I have airtight alibis in both cases. The first time I was with you, and the second time I was indulging in a rather satisfying dream till your screams woke me up."

"That's your story and you're sticking to it, right?"

"What do you mean by that?"

"Well . . . it is possible you could have come in here to go through my notes, escaped through my window to throw me off the scent, used the veranda to get back in through your own window, then taken off your costume and charged back in here to rescue me . . ." She tilted her small chin in defiance.

Her wild accusation took him so much by surprise that he erupted in a burst of laughter. "My dear girl, you've got bats in your belfry if you really believe that nonsense."

"Of course I don't really believe that. It's as stupid as your idea that someone's trying to steal my research. But you're making me crazy with all this cloak and dagger stuff . . ." she tailed off lamely.

He kept watching her, an unfathomable expression

in his blue eyes. Suddenly she felt much too self-conscious in the dense silence, acutely aware that they were all alone, sitting on her bed in the middle of the night, having this bizarre conversation.

And once again one of them was in a state of partial undress. Martin's loosely belted robe had sagged open, leaving his torso exposed. The sight of his broad shoulders and the fine mat of golden hair on his chest made her want to lean closer and delicately encircle each dark pink nipple with her tongue. *Julia, get a grip on yourself!*

Startled by her wanton thoughts, she looked up wide-eyed to find him still watching her. Through parted lips her breathing quickened. Under his gaze she felt naked, as if her flannel nightgown were as sheer as lace. A shiver of desire trembled through her, settling low in her hips with aching warmth. She could feel her breasts swell and tighten.

His gaze dwelt on her mouth for a moment, then slid lower until his eyes widened and she knew he could see the nipples hardening to telltale buds beneath the suddenly revealing flannel.

She jerked up onto her knees and lunged for the edge of the high bed with only one thought in mind. Escape. But her feet tangled in the jumbled sheets, pitching her face-first toward the pine-plank floor. With lightning reflexes, Martin reached out an arm and caught her, then set her back onto the bed, her knees still bent under her.

"Watch what you're doing, you'll hurt yourself." With a surprisingly soft touch, his hand pushed the tangled hair off her face.

"Wouldn't that make you happy after all those things I accused you of?" The words were almost a strangled sob.

For a breathless moment she stared into his stricken eyes. She wasn't sure who made the first move, but suddenly their lips met, hot and moist. Her body arched with a convulsive shudder and she tried to move backward, but his lips followed her, clinging hard to hers, his tongue exploring her mouth relentlessly.

Confused and overwhelmed by the torrent of new sensations assailing her, she felt his hard, muscled flesh beneath her hands and pushed, although she didn't know why. What she really wanted was to slide them around his body and feel his chest pressed intimately against her sensitive breasts, allowing him to feel the tight buds of her nipples through the soft flannel.

Trapped against the headboard, she felt his arms on either side of her, trembling slightly as they supported his weight. With a frustrated moan of desire, she turned her head aside, but his mouth followed, searching, his tongue thrusting deep, entwining with her own.

She'd never been kissed like this before, never felt this wild yearning before. Then suddenly she thought of Trudi. Was this kiss just another diversion to idle away his time? She shoved hard against his chest and felt him tense. Then with a groan he pushed himself away from her and sat up.

Turning away, he let out a long, shaky breath and ran a hand through his disheveled blond hair. "Julia, I'm sorry. I didn't mean for that to happen. After everything you've been through tonight."

The blood rushed to her face in a hot tidal wave and she felt the flush of passion in her cheeks deepen to burning shame. It wasn't Martin's fault. How could she have thrown herself at him with so little subtlety? Compared to her, Trudi seemed tame in her attempts to make Eric jealous. The tormenting comparison made her pull herself together in a desperate bid for composure.

"I'm sorry, too. Not to mention embarrassed." She gave a nervous little laugh. "I was as much to blame. People do the craziest things under the influence of shock, don't they?" Let him think her a babbling idiot, just so long as he didn't realize how he had affected her.

Martin turned back to her. "Look, it's late and you must be exhausted." He paused, and the silence vibrated with strain and awkwardness.

How the hell could he have behaved like that? He felt utterly disgusted by his lack of control. He'd never forced himself on a woman in his life. She'd had to push him away for God's sake. Worst of all, he'd wanted it to go on. She'd felt so good in his arms. His whole body responded to her in a way he'd never experienced before and it had taken him completely by surprise.

"I'll get out of here and let you get back to sleep."

"Yes, I'm very cranky unless I get my eight hours."

She was letting him off the hook, pretending they could just laugh it off. She was being so gallant it made him feel even more disgusted with himself.

He rose from the bed, went over to the window, and turned the catch that would prevent the casement from being raised. "This is locked now. I'm sure you'll be quite safe. If you need me, I'm right across the hall."

He turned back to Julia. She sat with her arms wrapped tightly around her knees, her violet eyes huge in her small pale face. With her looking so sweet and appealing, he wanted to dash back and take her into his arms again, cover her with tender, gentle kisses. But he wouldn't. He had to get the hell out of this room before he made a fool of himself, again.

"I'm sure everything will be fine. I'll see you in the morning." She gave him a bright smile.

He nodded gravely and walked out, closing the door quietly behind him.

Her false smile vanished and Julia let out her breath in a long, trembling sigh. She grabbed a pillow, clutching it tightly to her. Thank God he had come to his senses before she made an even bigger fool of herself.

Obviously she didn't excite him enough to make him lose control.

If she'd worried before about keeping her competitive edge just being friends with him, how on earth would she have managed had she slept with him?

The erotic images that thought conjured up drove her out of the bed as if it were made of nails. Feeling the need for activity, she began straightening the rumpled sheets and quilt. There wasn't much else she could do at a quarter to six in the morning. But the cold soon got her back under the covers. Not to sleep, of course. Who could sleep after the traumatic experiences she had been through?

The bright morning sun, shining full on her face, woke Julia from a deep, dreamless sleep. She struggled up onto her elbow to peer groggily at her travel alarm. Ten-thirty! Jerking up into sitting position, she brushed the tangled strands of auburn hair from her face. She never slept this late, not even on weekends. Then the events of the night before came crowding back into her head and she fell against the pillows with a groan.

How on earth could she face him this morning?

But she didn't have to. By the time she came down to breakfast half an hour later Martin had gone off to Fort Erie for the day and wasn't expected back until dinner.

Amy didn't mention anything about the intruder the night before, so obviously he hadn't filled her in on the latest break-in. Julia was happy to leave it that way. Somehow she felt reluctant to worry her further.

After downing a cup of coffee and a slice of toast, she hurried off to the archives to see Eric. *Forget about Martin and concentrate on the story*, she told herself, but that was easier said than done.

She had been turning over Martin's suggestion in her mind, but in the light of day it seemed even more ludicrous to think someone was after her information. There was nothing in her notes that anyone else couldn't go and find out for himself. Martin had admitted as much. After all, she wasn't infiltrating Colombian drug cartels or investigating a conspiracy to overthrow the government, as he had done. All those years of living on the edge of danger had led him to make intrigue out of mere coincidence.

When she entered the small storefront office of the *Gleaner*, Eric was sitting at the cluttered desk, the phone cradled on his shoulder.

"How naive can you be? Men like him are only interested in one thing . . ." He looked up and colored self-consciously. ". . . Look, I can't talk now. I've got to go. I'll see you at lunch." He put down the phone and turned to her with a flustered smile.

"I'm sorry, I didn't mean to interrupt your call," she said awkwardly and shut the door behind her.

Eric clearly hadn't calmed down since that awful scene in the diner. His wiry red curls stood on end as if he'd been raking his hands through them, and under the pretense of a smile he looked so miserable that Julia felt heartily sorry for him.

"Not at all, not at all." He stood abruptly, knocking his chair over. "It is I who should apologize to you for last night." He righted the swiveling desk chair and stood clutching the back.

"That's quite all right," Julia mumbled uncomfortably. That was the last thing she wanted to talk about, because she couldn't avoid thinking about the aftermath. That argument on the way home. Martin making her acknowledge that she was jealous.

Eric cleared his throat and his eyes slid away from hers. "I suppose you must have guessed by now how things stand between Trudi and me."

"No . . . no, I didn't really . . ." She felt intensely embarrassed.

"I feel I owe you an explanation after my shabby behavior." He clearly needed to unburden himself, and somehow Julia's heart went out to him. "Trudi and I have been seeing each other for the past five years now. We have an understanding, if you know what I mean . . ."

"Yes, Trudi did say something about that to me."

"She did?" He blinked in surprise.

"She talks about you a lot, you know."

Julia saw a flicker of hope cross his face and felt the strongest urge to reassure him that Martin posed no real threat. Even as an imaginary rival though, he must be pretty daunting. Heaven knows, she could sympathize with Eric's jealousy. She knew that torment much too well. But it was none of her business. It was up to Eric and Trudi to work out their problems, and she had a feeling that once Martin was gone it would happen by itself.

". . . We *are* going to be married as soon as I can afford it, and my prospects are beginning to look brighter by the moment." In spite of his optimistic words he looked anxious, as if he hadn't quite convinced himself. He picked at the gray tweed chair back with nervous fingers.

"Well, that's just wonderful. I wish you all the luck in the world." Although reluctant to get involved, she wanted to reassure him a little more.

". . . And I'm sure you'll be happy to know that I'm close to wrapping up the story, so I'll be out of your hair soon. And then you can concentrate on patching things up with Trudi."

And Martin will be gone, she wanted to add, but Eric must have gotten the message because he seemed to brighten at her words.

"Well, enough of my problems, what can I do to help you today?" He began shuffling and stacking the papers on his desk with quick, excitable motions.

"What do you know about Titus Flynn?"

He whistled and his wiry eyebrows shot up. "Where did you hear about Titus Flynn?"

"I'm interested in the smuggling and black marketeering that went on during the war. One of the books in the library mentioned his name."

Eric came around his desk and perched close to her on the edge. In a furtive gesture he looked behind him and she found herself looking uneasily over her own shoulder.

"Folks around here said he was the leader of a huge smuggling ring that brought in everything from rum to escaping slaves. Unfortunately for those poor blacks, trusting Titus Flynn was as good as putting your faith in the devil. He would take their money, then turn them in to the bounty hunters for an even greater sum."

With a tingle of anticipation, Julia took out her notebook and started to write. Ever since she saw him mentioned as the leader of the local black marketeers, she'd had a suspicion he might have been involved in the robbery.

It was almost too far-fetched that he could be the one. After all, smuggling was a brisk trade in those days, and many people were involved. But somehow she couldn't let go of the possible connection. Besides, what would it hurt? Another colorful local figure to add to her story.

"What happened to him?"

"No one knows. He vanished a few days before the American occupation of the town and was never heard from again."

The same time as the paywagon had been stolen. She felt a little shiver. "But he owned a farm around here, didn't he?"

"Yes, but it burned to the ground during the American retreat, just like the rest of the town."

"Do you know where it was?"

"No, I don't. Is it important?"

She shrugged. "I'm not sure, but it might be. Do you think we could find out?"

"The library has all the land claims records on microfiche. I'm pretty sure Flynn was an original settler. His deed should be on file. I'll dig it up for you, shall I?" Eric's eyes shone with interest, and suddenly it seemed his worries were forgotten.

Julia remembered Trudi's telling her how Eric hankered after the glamour of big-city reporting. She'd seen the *Niagara Gleaner* and Trudi hadn't been exaggerating. With reports on social events and new store openings, it was little more than a puff sheet for the town. Eric was probably at the mercy of his advertisers not to print anything uncomplimentary and dying to sink his teeth into something interesting.

"Thanks, Eric," Julia said warmly, feeling glad she'd helped take his mind off his troubles with Trudi. "I'll keep you posted."

Yes, she was in the perfect mood for this place, Julia thought, lonesome and melancholy. And it had nothing to do with Martin's not being there. It was just the weather.

Lowering slate-colored clouds had rolled in just after lunch, obliterating the sun, chilling her to the bone as she wandered through the old churchyard. The winter light grayed and blended the colors of the thick pines with the cold dark earth, the frozen brown turf. Odd gusts of wind went moaning through the ancient cedars and the twisted oaks, picking up the dead leaves to send them swirling around her feet and rattling against the gravestones.

When she had first arrived, a school group had been noisily tramping around, teenagers giggling and yelling to each other. Their youth and exuberance contrasted painfully with the reminders of mortality, and they seemed oblivious to the things Julia found so touching.

But they had gone now and left her to the peace and serenity. Crows cawed in the pines, the wind picked up, sighing through the bare oaks, carrying the sound of the courthouse clock chiming four.

How wonderful to be alone, to think, to dream . . . to wonder where he was. For the hundredth time today she dragged her thoughts away from Martin, back to the article that should be the most important thing on her mind right now.

This confusion was driving her crazy. She stopped and took a deep breath, inhaling the smell of the earth, savoring the peace and serenity, desperate to absorb some of this tranquillity inside her and stop the turmoil of thoughts and emotions. She no longer knew how to respond to him. He disturbed her in a far more complex way than he had ever done before. As complex as her feelings had become toward him.

But what were her feelings? She wasn't in love with him, she knew that for sure.

Near the center of the churchyard, beneath a sparse old fir, stood a small crypt built from massive blocks of gray stone. Julia stood on the step and peered through the rusting wrought-iron doorway, framed by limestone columns, into the marble interior. From the names and dates, she guessed that two couples must be buried inside. Straining her eyes in the gloom, she could just make out the lines of an inscription cut into the white marble between the vaults.

Until the day breaks and the shadows flee away
And with the morn those angel faces smile
Which I have loved long since and lost awhile.

Julia's throat tightened and her eyes filled with tears. She gripped the curving wrought iron more tightly and leaned her head on the grill. Time was so short, so fleeting. Was she making the most of hers? These people had lived and loved and suffered and had been happy. Was she happy?

Yes, her life was very fulfilling. She had the satisfaction of being independent, knowing she could make it on her own. And yet, wouldn't life be sweeter if she had someone to share it with?

A crow flew overhead, cawing loudly, and settled in a nearby tree. The raucous cry brought Julia out of her self-absorption. She was here to work, she reminded herself sharply and took out her pad to write down the inscription.

As the last echo of the cawing died away, the silence settled around her. The sighing of the wind only served to intensify the utter quiet. Suddenly she realized there was no sign or sound of any other person, and the gloomy, gray winter light had begun to deepen around her. It was time to be going back to the cheerful warmth of the George.

The wind whistled through the broken stained-glass window in the crypt, sounding like a human sigh. She shivered. Were there really ghosts? No, there couldn't be. But then, how could that vital energy that gave a human being the breath of life be extinguished?

Suddenly, scenes from *Night of the Living Dead* began unreeling in grotesque detail in her mind. She tried to laugh away her fanciful thoughts, but somehow, right now, she wanted to get the hell out of this graveyard.

Julia turned to leave and almost walked into a dark figure standing right behind her.

A scream of terror tore from her throat. She hauled off blindly and threw a punch. Her bunched up fist connected with flesh and bone, sending the surprisingly substantial ghoul to lie in a sprawling heap on the frozen grass at the foot of a massive granite urn a yard away. Then she turned and bolted.

"For God's sake, Julia, you could have just *told* me to go away."

Martin's voice penetrated the unreasoning terror and brought her to a skidding halt. Gasping with the effort to catch her breath and get her galloping heartbeat under control, she turned and focused on the man now struggling up to a sitting position on the ground. With one hand clamped to his left jaw, he stared up at her in complete amazement.

The intensity of her relief to see it was only Martin brought her running to his side and she helped him to his feet.

"Martin, I'm sorry, did I hurt you? You shouldn't sneak up on people like that. You scared me half to death!" She brushed ineffectually at the dead leaves and dirt clinging to his navy coat.

"Believe me, I'll certainly remember for next time." He grinned and winced, gingerly working his jaw. "I thought you heard me coming."

Noticing the angry red mark on his chin, Julia became aware of the pain in her knuckles and felt sick with guilt. She must have really hurt him. "I'm so sorry. I didn't mean to do that."

He rubbed his jaw. "It's all right. I probably deserved it. I'm sure you've been wanting to take a swing at me for a long time," he grinned.

"Well . . . only when I first met you." Julia gave a small reluctant smile, then bit her lip. There had been moments . . . But she still felt distressed to think she'd actually hit him.

"For someone who looks so fragile, you pack quite a punch," he said with an ironic chuckle. "I'd hate to think of the damage you could cause if you meant it."

"Serves you right for sneaking up on me." She slanted him an impudent look.

"I didn't sneak up on you. You were just too engrossed to hear me." He glanced at the small crypt, then back to her. "Crying over long-dead people again, Julia?"

There was no mockery in his gentle voice, and she had to turn away from the probing intensity in his eyes. Her emotions were in a confused jumble that tugged her in too many directions at once. This wasn't how she'd expected the conversation to go in their first meeting after last night.

He'd given no indication he even remembered last night. Why should she be surprised? It was obvious that kissing her hadn't been an earth-shattering experience for him. But he had made her want to abandon herself to the erotic pleasure skyrocketing through her at the touch of his lips. Just thinking about the way she'd responded made her burn with embarrassment.

"What are you doing here anyway?" she said quickly, anxious to change the subject. "I thought you were in Fort Erie?"

"I came back." He grinned and rubbed his jaw. The red patch was now turning purplish blue. "You obviously missed me."

"But I didn't miss you, did I?" She nodded toward the bruise with a penitent grimace.

He laughed out loud and she couldn't help joining in. Once again the buzzing excitement she always felt in his presence tingled through her veins like fine wine, but it was clear she didn't have the same effect on him. And that sobering truth kept her anchored to reality.

"Ow! . . . that's cold!" Martin flinched back from the small package of frozen peas Julia held against his bruised jaw.

"Of course it's cold, but it'll help, so leave it there," she commanded and sat down on the wooden chair beside him in Amy's big modern restaurant kitchen.

He dutifully obeyed and held the icy plastic in place.

The throbbing pain had begun to ease. "Where did you learn to punch like that anyway?"

"From my dad. In his younger days he held the Canadian Forces middleweight championship."

"So that's where that sergeant-major routine comes from."

"Just major, thank you." Her full mouth curved in a wry smile.

"Yes, sir," he grinned. "You probably didn't need my help last night. That guy doesn't know how close he came to being pulverized." His skin was beginning to freeze. He put the package of peas down on the pine table.

"I . . . didn't get a chance to do it last night, but I meant to thank you for your help . . ." Julia's voice trailed off awkwardly and she didn't quite meet his eyes.

"Judging by your right hook, you could have managed just fine without it."

And maybe she'd have been better off using it on him last night. What had possessed him, taking advantage of the situation like that? What did it take to drum it into his head that she wasn't interested? If he needed any confirmation, the way she had pushed him away spoke louder than words. He gingerly touched his fingertips to the tender spot on his jaw, suppressing a wince at the dull throb of pain.

With a soft sigh, Julia gently reached out and covered his jaw with her warm palm. He closed his hand over hers and held it against his face for a moment and once again felt that intense surge of protectiveness that had shot through him last night when he thought she was in danger.

He'd spent a few wakeful hours analyzing that one. Why her? Of all the female journalists he'd worked with, in situations that made this look like a Sunday school picnic, he'd never felt any particular need to protect them, no more than he would any other colleague. He came back to the present abruptly as he felt her slide her hand slowly out of his.

Julia turned away, confused by the look in his eyes, by the tenderness that had passed between them. Or had she been mistaken? She wasn't very good at figuring him out.

Martin stopped her with a hand on her shoulder, forcing her to face him. "I'm glad I was there."

The absolute sincerity in his voice and the earnest expression in his eyes as they sought hers made her feel as if she mattered to him. But he would have done the same for anyone, logic told her, because she had begun to realize he was a man who cared about people.

Now that she'd put aside her antagonism and begun to know him, she could see Martin wasn't the type of man who could stand by and not get involved because it wasn't his business. He'd be the type to wade in and defend anyone in trouble. Even her.

"Speaking of that guy last night, what are you going to do about him?"

"What can I do?" Julia picked up the makeshift ice pack and handed it to Martin, who held it to his jaw again. "I don't particularly feel like reporting it to the police. What am I going to say? Someone dressed up in an old uniform and broke into my room just to steal my briefcase? I can imagine what they'd think of that story."

"You have a point there." He sighed, settling his long limbs more comfortably in the old wooden pressback chair. His knee brushed against hers. "On the other hand, we can't just ignore it either."

"I still can't believe he was after something in my notes." Julia forced herself to concentrate on the serious business at hand, but she had missed him all day long and now she just wanted to fill her eyes with him. "I've discovered from talking to people that there's a real problem with burglaries in this town. It's not as idyllic as it looks."

"Believe what you want, I still think there's something dodgy going on and I intend to keep my eye on you."

"Don't blame me if it turns out to be a colossal waste of your time."

Try as she might to sound unconcerned, inside her a tiny nugget of warmth began to spread. It would be dangerous to allow herself to get used to the attention, to rely on it. She preferred to rely on herself.

His eyes twinkled with wickedness. "At the very least I might discover what fascinating material you've uncovered."

"It shouldn't surprise me that even your chivalrous impulses have an ulterior motive." She shot him an arch look. "Two can play at that game. You can bet I'll be keeping my eye on you, too."

"I'm counting on it." The daring sparkle lighting up her face made him feel lighthearted. He laughed softly and held her gaze, wanting to drown in those violet depths. "Do you have the guts to defy destiny, Julia?"

NINE

There it was on her right-hand side, just as Amy said it would be—a big green barn with MCKINLEY AND SONS HOLSTEINS emblazoned in bold black letters. But it was hardly just across the road from the Balfour place. More like a quarter of a mile up a rutted twisting lane. But it meant the approach to the Balfour farm should be coming up soon on her left.

And there it was. She turned off onto a narrow dirt road edged on both sides by massive trees, bare of leaves, dark and twisted against the leaden gray sky.

In the twenty minutes since she'd left town, the wind had picked up and the lowering clouds gathered until they seemed to sit right on top of the bare orchards and frozen brown fields crouching on either side of the narrow concession roads.

She'd be glad to reach the house. Even if it was some musty old Victorian horror, at least it would be a warm haven from the wind. Amy had told her the old house was in frequent use by the family as a weekend retreat.

And she also couldn't wait to get a look at the material Jim's late Uncle Harry had collected in his role as the Balfour family historian. It would make a wonderful background to her story if she could find out something about the flesh and blood people who had lived through that time, people her readers could care about.

She'd asked Amy why all these important historical documents weren't in the archives where they belonged.

Amy had chuckled. "Uncle Harry was an ornery old coot. He'd taken a dislike to Eric and said he nagged him about the stuff all the time. He said that Eric could darn well wait until he was dead before he got his hands on them. I've been meaning to see to that myself, but I've just been too busy."

The wind was truly howling now, shaking her car with its force, and the first icy pellets spattered against the windshield as she rounded the final turn and caught sight of a little house nestled in the trees. With clapboard siding painted a wedgewood green and freshly trimmed in white and dormer windows studding the steeply pitched roof, it bore no resemblance to the spooky old Ontario gothic she'd almost expected.

Julia stepped inside, stamping off the snow and shedding her boots and coat. Glad of her cozy turquoise fleece-lined jumpsuit, she found the thermostat and turned up the heat to a comfortable level.

To one side of the front door, set conveniently beside a modern kitchen nook, stood a huge oak dining table. And on the other side, the massive chimney of a fieldstone fireplace formed a natural dividing wall with the other ground-floor room.

She absolutely adored this house, Julia decided, looking to the oriel window set high in the soaring cathedral ceiling of the other, smaller room.

Obeying her stomach's persistent grumbling, she searched the kitchen and found a box of crackers. Amy had told her she was welcome to help herself to food, although the cupboards might be a little bare. With a plateful of saltines and a can of pop from the fridge, she went into the smaller living room, over to the office area in the corner.

Uncle Harry had all the family papers neatly cataloged in a huge roll-top oak secretary and glass-fronted bookcases. As Amy had promised, she found Sarah Balfour's diary carefully laid away in a drawer.

Settling herself in a big old armchair by the window, Julia touched the fragile russet leather binding with reverent fingers and thought of the living, breathing girl who had committed her secret thoughts to this book.

She opened it to the first page of meticulous copperplate script and through almost two hundred years Sarah reached out and captured her heart.

Outside the Balfour farmhouse the wind whistled and howled through the trees, the snow had begun to fall, but she hardly noticed. With tears rolling down her cheeks, she read of the captain's last days and Sarah's desperation. Read her guilty, heartbreaking confession that she had fallen in love with her patient. But Frederick Fairfax was a married man, a man no power on earth could save.

Suddenly Julia sat up straight, her eyes moving avidly over the page. From his fevered ramblings, Sarah had pieced together the story of the captain's injuries. In the dead of night, a couple of miles upriver from Fort George, near the old smuggler's house . . .

She stopped reading with a gasp. A couple of miles upriver from Fort George? Those remains were found a couple of miles upriver. Could the old smuggler be Titus Flynn?

She continued reading.

The captain had come upon a group of men hauling kettles filled with silver coins up the steep riverbank to a waiting wagon. Fairfax and his lieutenant, Oakshott, rode in to arrest the thieves, Titus Flynn and four others, high-ranking officers from both sides.

But tragedy had struck. The treacherous Oakshott

opened fire, killing everyone and leaving Fairfax for dead, before escaping with the wagon full of silver.

Julia let out another gasp. This was it. It had to be the story of those pitiful bones. But there was only one way to know for sure—finding the site of Titus's farm—because that was where Fairfax found the conspirators.

Her gaze flew avidly back to the page and she felt a lump in her throat as she read how the captain had stumbled into the inn, covered in blood, mere minutes ahead of the invading American soldiers. How they had hidden him in the cellar, how Sarah had nursed him for two weeks until his tragic death. Julia could almost smell the cool earth walls of the cellar, hear the captain's fevered groans, Sarah's heartbroken weeping.

A heavy pounding on the door made her nearly jump out of her skin. With a gasp, she put a hand to her thudding heart. Absorbed in the story, she hadn't even been aware that she had been squinting to read the pages in the gathering gloom of late afternoon or that the snow now blew so thickly she could barely see the trees outside.

Who could be out there, miles from anywhere, in a raging snowstorm? Moving slowly toward the door, she thought of the intruder in her room and her heartbeat quickened to a mad gallop. Lifting the lace curtain covering the small square window, she saw a dark hooded figure in a familiar navy parka huddled against the wind.

Julia turned the lock and opened the door. Martin stumbled in with a screaming gust of wind and a flurry of powdery white snow, then helped her battle to close the door against the blast.

"What are you doing here?"

"I came because I was worried about you. Are you going to hit me again?"

From beneath the hood he tried to smile through chattering teeth, but she could see he was shivering and obviously frozen. His nose and cheeks were red from the cold and ice still clung to his eyebrows. The bruise on his chin had deepened to a livid purplish yellow against his pale, chilled skin.

"Don't be ridiculous," she said briskly, but her heart gave a traitorous jolt. Did that mean that he cared?

While Martin hung his coat on the rack and pulled off his boots, she stared out through the swirling snow, barely able to see past the front of the house.

"But how did you know I was here? And how did you get here?" Her own car was already nearly covered by a drift and she saw no sign of his.

"Amy told me. Now do you mind if I get warm first before you give me the third degree?" He swiped at the snow still clinging to his damp navy corduroy trousers.

The light was failing fast. Shadows filled the corners and made the outlines of the worn, comfortable furnishings indistinct. Julia flicked the wall switch and the soft glow of an old brass candelabra illuminated the oak dining table.

"I don't suppose there's something hot to drink around here?"

"I guess I could see if there's some coffee." She went into the kitchen nook tucked into a corner by the stairs and found a jar of instant.

When the coffee was ready, she went into the smaller living area and found Martin had lit the fire laid ready in the hearth.

Putting his mug on the hearthstones, she perched on the arm of the couch clutching her own cup, watching him kneel by the fireplace stacking on more logs to build up the blaze. She waited for an explanation. What was he doing here in the middle of a snowstorm? Did he fall from the sky? She couldn't believe this man.

But as the wood caught and burned brighter, Julia found herself thinking how wonderful he looked kneeling there, the firelight bathing the chiseled planes of his face in a warm glow and gleaming on his damp, tousled blond hair.

In the flickering light his heavy ski sweater glowed ruby red, and the horizontal band of navy and white snowflakes accentuated the strength of his broad shoulders. The aura of masculinity she'd once found so intimidating now drew her like the warmth of the flames.

He stood, turning his back to the fire and answered her inquiring stare. "I walked," he said calmly, taking a sip from his steaming mug.

"From the George?"

"No, from the end of the driveway. It's completely blocked. And I came because I was worried about you. The forecast says it's going to get much worse. Thought you might be nervous having to stay out here by yourself, or worse still be foolhardy enough to try making it back." He sounded as though he wouldn't put anything past her.

Draining his cup, he put it on the mantel and held out his hands to the blaze as Julia realized what this would mean. A winter storm in Toronto could be dangerous enough, but out here, on the lonely farmlands of the exposed Niagara Peninsula, driving through a blizzard would be insane. She wouldn't risk freezing to death in a ditch just to avoid being stranded here overnight. So face the facts, she'd have to stay the night here. With Martin. She gulped in dismay.

He turned back to her. "While I'm here I'd like to take a look at the family papers. I know this violates the terms of our agreement, but under the circumstances maybe you'd be prepared to bend the rules."

At his coaxing smile Julia shook her head, the corners of her mouth curving with amusement. "Somehow I just knew there'd be an ulterior motive for this knight in shining armor routine . . . Okay, be my guest." With a mock bow she waved toward the office area in the corner of the room.

Sinking back down into the chair, Julia tried to resume reading the diary, but somehow it didn't hold her attention the way it had before.

It was past five and quite dark outside now. The room looked completely different, with a cozy fire crackling in the hearth, lamps casting pools of yellow light, and Martin. Most of all, Martin. He sat at the desk, his tortoiseshell-rimmed glasses on, absorbed in the papers before him and taking notes.

Julia toyed with the zipper tab of her jumpsuit as her gaze kept sliding over toward him, noticing every little mannerism, the way he absently lifted silky strands of hair off his forehead with the pencil, then tapped it against his mouth. Her eyes traced the shape of his lips and remembered how they had felt on hers.

She squirmed in the chair and quickly looked down at the diary, then realized she'd been staring at the same page for half an hour and hadn't absorbed a word.

Shutting the book with a snap, she rose to her feet, feeling restless. Martin looked up to shoot her a faraway, absentminded smile, then went back to his reading. Julia drifted upstairs, wondering about the sleeping arrangements. She shouldn't be feeling so nervous and awkward. She had nothing to worry about. After all, look at him, perfectly relaxed and at ease, not like a man planning a seduction scene. Why did the thought even cross her mind? It obviously hadn't crossed his.

At the top of the stairs she flicked on the light and looked around in dismay at the large loft with three dormer windows, a single bed set into each alcove. They'd have to share the room, unless one of them slept on the small two-seater couch, and she'd just look silly insisting on that.

But despite her awkwardness, she was glad he had turned up. Spending the night here all alone would have been unnerving. She had to be mature about the situation.

A door on her left led into a large bathroom, complete with an old-fashioned claw-footed tub, and there was a further room beyond. Another bedroom, she noticed with relief, and walked across the wide pine boards to flop down on the big old-fashioned brass bed. She lay back on the blue log cabin quilt and sighed. It felt as comfortable as it looked.

"I see you found your room."

At the sound of Martin's voice from the doorway behind her, Julia jerked up to a sitting position, then jumped to her feet, smoothing a hand self-consciously over her French braid.

Silhouetted by the light spilling out from the bathroom behind him, he lounged against the door frame with his hands in his pockets and smiled at her.

"Isn't this a charming little place? From the moment I saw it I felt very comfortable here. I was almost tempted to ask Amy if she was interested in selling it."

He walked into the room to peer through the window on the other side of the bed, into the mass of swirling flakes faintly tapping against the glass.

"But then I came to my senses. What would I want, being tied to a place, worrying about gas bills and mowing the lawn? And all those interminable responsibilities that go along with settling down." He turned and smiled at her, that devastating boyish grin she found so hard to resist.

She had no right to feel this terrible sense of disappointment. After all, he'd made no secret of how he felt about permanence. But she had to say something. "You've been here before?"

Martin nodded. "The other day. And by the way, if you're looking for Fairfax's diary, don't bother. I have it. You'll just have to wait your turn," he said with a wry quirk to his lips.

She laughed. "That's fine. I have first dibs on Sarah's."

"So we're even then." He smiled into her eyes and then something warm and unsettling mingled with that smile. "Don't you think this is a wonderful little country hideaway just perfect for two?"

Julia unconsciously glanced down at the bed and suddenly had a vivid picture of herself, naked and warm in Martin's arms, his body molded to hers. Her heart started beating faster and she felt suddenly breathless.

She quickly looked up and caught him watching her with a tiny smile in his disturbing blue eyes, before they too quickly dropped to the bed, then back up again. Her cheeks began to burn. He probably had a pretty good idea what was going through her head.

"Well, I'm starved." She tried to sound brisk and businesslike, but she could feel her face getting even hotter. Julia swallowed hard, much too aware of his vibrant masculine presence filling the shadowy room, the awareness crackling between them across the bed.

"Me, too."

His voice was soft and husky and fraught with unmistakable meaning, his eyes sliding down to the bed, then slowly back up her body, a small wicked smile in their depths. She knew very well he wasn't referring to food.

Clearly the same thought had occurred to him, too, but for very different reasons. For her, making love would be an emotional response to the way she felt about him, but she knew he would merely be satisfying a physical urge.

"Yes . . . well." She struggled hard to sound matter-of-fact. "Why don't I go downstairs and see what I can find for dinner."

"I have a few suggestions." The sultry intonation in his voice sent a small shiver racing through her.

She didn't want to touch that one with a ten-foot pole. Julia headed for the door, the bright lights, and safety. "In that case, you get to be the chef and I'll help,'' she said, resolutely refusing to play his teasing little game.

As he followed her through the bathroom, she heard his soft chuckle behind her and his low, husky voice. ''Coward.''

The tiny kitchen seemed suddenly even smaller as they searched for the makings of a meal. The harder she tried to avoid Martin, the more she seemed to keep bumping into him.

''There's only some rice here in the cupboard,'' Julia stepped back and felt her hip brush against his with an electrical jolt. She moved away abruptly and turned to see him holding up a frosty plastic bag in triumph.

''Then we have a meal, because I found some frozen vegetables.''

Julia wrinkled her nose. ''That doesn't sound very appetizing.''

''Just you wait.'' With a little lift of his eyebrows he flashed her a wicked grin. ''I have a way with frozen vegetables you wouldn't believe.''

By the time the rice was done, Martin had whipped up a stir-fry, and they sat down to eat at one end of the large dining table.

Julia took a mouthful of the spicy concoction. ''Mmm . . . Not bad.''

''Compared to some of the things I've had to eat in my travels, this is a banquet. I remember once in Africa . . .''

''Please.'' She held up her hand with a grin. ''Not the elephant story again. I'd like to enjoy this meal.''

He laughed and began to eat. By the time they had finished they were chatting comfortably about inconsequential things. *Like old friends,* Julia found herself thinking while she made the coffee. How oddly domestic this whole scene felt.

She carried their cups into the living room to find Martin sitting on the floor in front of the fire, long legs stretched out in front of him, his back against the old chintz sofa. Set on a thick oriental carpet and flanked by easy chairs on either side, it made a cozy little nook in the large room.

In the warmth of the fire he had discarded his heavy sweater and pushed up the sleeves of the navy cotton turtleneck to expose strong forearms dusted with dark blond hair. He took the cup from her hand and patted the carpet beside him with a companionable smile.

Julia sat down next to him and sipped her coffee, staring into the flames, feeling comfortable, despite the silence. It would be much too easy to get used to this.

Had it only been a few days ago she'd stood there in Roger's office and felt like strangling him? No, she'd been far more specific in her diabolical plans. She began to giggle.

He turned to look at her with a quizzical expression that made her giggle harder. "Care to share the joke?"

"The Porkers Stern," she finally gasped out.

"Yes, Julia . . . that's hilarious." He gave her a mystified smile. "Just what have you got in your coffee?"

"When you were reminding Roger that you were in The Porkers Stern when the story idea came to you, I have to confess that's exactly where I wanted to stuff you."

Martin threw back his head and laughed. "And I thought you were only contemplating murder."

Their laughter slowly died away. "I can't believe that was only a week ago." Julia shook her head. "You had me so intimidated with all your experience, and the way Roger praised you to the skies, but I had to stand up for myself."

"I had *you* intimidated. The way you looked down your aristocratic nose at me, I always felt you were comparing me to that rich boyfriend of yours. And worse, that I didn't measure up to your standards.'' He gave her a rueful smile.

Julia stared at him aghast. To think that Martin, who was usually so right on the mark, could have misinterpreted her insecurity and shyness so completely.

''Believe me, nothing could be farther from the truth. If I gave you that impression, I'm so sorry. Martin, I don't know what to say, I feel terrible.''

''Well, don't. I guess I was being oversensitive. The truth of the matter, my dear, is that you dented my ego a little and I didn't like it.'' He stared down into his coffee. ''I tried to tell myself it didn't matter, but it did, and that's the bottom line.'' Looking back up at her again, his face held a sober expression she didn't often see that left her unsure of how to reply.

His admission jolted her. Did that mean he'd been interested in her from the start?

''I know you must have guessed, but Brian isn't my boyfriend anymore. We broke up a month ago.'' That wasn't what she meant to say at all, but somehow the words just slipped out.

''Do you want to talk about it?'' he asked, quiet and compassionate.

She shook her head, ''I wouldn't want to bore you.''

''Hey, I thought we were friends. You don't have to tell me if you don't want to. But I find that sometimes it helps . . .''

He turned to gaze into the fire, cradling the coffee mug between his long fingers while Julia drank her fill of his strong profile. She traced the outline of his smooth forehead, the straight nose, lingered for a moment on the finely modeled curve of his lips with their hint of sensuality, the firm sweep of his jaw. He turned his head and she met his eyes, unable to tear her gaze away from the warmth and perception she saw there.

''He asked me to marry him.'' The words came out of nowhere, and suddenly she realized that it didn't matter. None of it mattered. Brian didn't matter anymore.

But Martin shifted, turning slightly toward her, and murmured, "Go on."

With a sigh she continued, "Brian had everything I'd want in a husband. He believed in the importance of stability. He planned to build a career in his father's law firm, and he wanted us to raise a family in the same neighborhood where he grew up. It all sounded so wonderful to me. You see, as a child I never really had a permanent home. Making a home and putting down roots is very important to me, and that's what I thought I'd found with Brian. But there was only one thing missing. He didn't love me. But he appreciated me," she smiled wryly. "He told me I would be the perfect wife for a prominent lawyer, a wife he could be proud of. But that wasn't enough for me."

"I'm glad to hear it." Martin set his mug down on the end table beside him and took her hand lightly in his, playing with her fingers, his touch making her heartbeat become suddenly erratic. "Don't ever settle for anything less than what you need. He sounds like a pompous twit who obviously doesn't deserve you anyway, because you're sweet and vulnerable, caring and honest."

Julia looked down at her hand in his with a nervous laugh. He was being so serious. Martin, who usually took things so lightly.

"You make me sound like a Boy Scout." She lifted her gaze to his face, but he wasn't smiling. Something in his expression made her catch her breath.

He leaned forward and his lips softly touched hers. Swept with a wave of emotion, she started back for a fraction of a second before gently returning the pressure. His lips brushed over hers with dizzying, tantalizing delicacy. Then he kissed the corner of her mouth and she turned her head, seeking the warmth of his mouth with her softly parted lips.

He took a deep shuddering breath, gathering her into his arms in one strong, possessive gesture and Julia went willingly. No longer tentative, his mouth claimed hers with hungry passion. She clung to him, wrapping her arms tightly around him, unable to get close enough.

He gently lowered her to the carpet and she trembled, feeling the hard, muscled length of his body fitting so intimately, so perfectly, against her own. The kiss deepened, slowed, became hot and intense, his mouth taking hers more completely, teaching her the infinitely sweet erotic possibilities of a kiss, making her melt under him.

The room fell quiet, the silence punctuated by the crackle of logs on the fire and soft, mingled murmurs of pleasure. She felt his fingers at her throat, her jumpsuit zipper slowly being lowered, and held her breath.

Then she felt the slow, arousing touch of his lean fingers caressing her breast through the flimsy lace covering. With a soft moan she arched against him, weak with pleasure and wanting more.

At her response his mouth became suddenly fierce and demanding, stirring a primitive hunger she had never known before. Desperate to touch him, she dragged up the thin cotton sweater and slipped her hand beneath, smoothing it over the bare flesh of his back, running it through the soft hairs on his muscled chest with trembling, inexpert caresses.

With a small moan, his lips left hers and he stared down into her dazed face for a moment.

"Do you know how much I want you, Julia?" His breath came rapidly, his eyes dark and burning with desire.

Then she felt the heat of his mouth on her skin, kissing a shivering path of ecstasy down her neck, nuzzling the hollow at the base of her throat, then over the swell of her breasts.

He paused and lifted his head. Through hazy eyes she watched him undo the front closure of her bra and carefully move the lace aside to gaze down at her bare breast, at the rosy nipple taut and straining to be taken by him. She could feel his hot, moist breath on her naked skin and arched toward his parted lips, needing him with a desperation that was close to madness.

With tantalizing deliberation he lowered his head, until she could feel him slowly draw her nipple into the silky heat of his mouth and send a wave of breathtaking pleasure flooding through her, turning her limbs to water.

Her head dropped back and she closed her eyes with a shuddering gasp. "Oh, Martin . . ." Abandoning herself to the melting need deep inside, she wrapped one leg around his waist and urged her hips against him.

Her small whimpered moans of pleasure, the taste of her in his mouth, and the feeling of her warm softness moving so erotically against his belly were driving him swiftly past the point of no return.

But from the moment she had sought his mouth with her own, he'd been lost. He was mad for her, greedy and reckless and desperate to fill his senses with her. Every movement became teasing, exquisite torture as her slender thigh pressed between his own, rubbing against him until he felt so hard and tight he was afraid he'd go over the edge at any second.

With shaking hands, he pushed the jumpsuit down over her shoulders. She pulled her arms from the sleeves and he felt her hands fumble for his belt, the brush of her fingers over his stomach sending a rush of hard, hot desire arrowing through his loins.

He dragged the jumpsuit down over her hips, along with her underwear. But he couldn't bear to stop kissing her, hot and urgent, his tongue plunging into her luscious, tender mouth. He ran a hand obsessively over the smooth curves of her bare skin, her flat belly, the downy softness below. His hand slid gently between her thighs, into even softer flesh, warm, wet silk between his fingers. She gave a frantic gasp against his mouth and shuddered.

Oh God, she was so sweet, so beautiful. He needed to bury himself in her sweetness, her softness, feel her surrounding him.

He felt her urgently tugging at his waistband and helped her push his clothes out of the way. The feeling of her cool, slender hand closing around his burning flesh was almost more than he could bear. Intolerable pleasure and frantic hunger consumed him.

"Now, darling. Please," she cried softly. Then she was guiding him inside and he slid into her luxuriant warmth with an agonized sigh of relief.

Yet not relief, not yet. Impossible to be more aroused, but the hunger that tore at him intensified as he heard her gasp of pleasure and felt her bare leg wind around him, allowing him to plunge more deeply into her. Some distant, rational part of him realized she must have gotten one leg free from her jumpsuit.

With every movement, every voluptuous, unrestrained response of her body to his, he felt his release threatening to overtake him like a tidal wave. He couldn't hold on much longer. But he wanted to give her everything. Make it perfect.

He slid his hands under her firm, rounded bottom, raised her hips to nestle even closer to his, and began moving against her in a slow circular motion.

Julia gasped out his name and wrapped her arms around him more tightly. Her flesh burned for him, and pleasure rocked her senses. She loved the feeling of him moving inside her and moaned in desperation as the wild intense pressure kept building until she almost couldn't bear it. Every touch of his hands, his skin, his mouth pushed her farther into the frantic spiral and then suddenly it was on her.

A rush of exquisite release went shuddering through her as she clutched at his shoulders and cried out his name. With an inarticulate gasp, he buried his head against her neck and she felt him move convulsively in her arms as his own release came.

They clung to each other, panting, slowly descending from the pinnacle, as she felt the rapid thud of his heartbeat slowing down. Pure, sublime happiness overwhelmed her. Nothing could be more intimate, more perfect, than this moment.

She raised a trembling hand to his head, still buried in her neck, and stroked his damp hair, feeling the erratic rhythm of his breathing begin to slow, feeling the strength of him as he strove to bring control back over his body.

He rolled over onto his back, and she felt bereft at breaking their physical union. But then he smiled at her, gathering her close, and she nestled in against his shoulder in dazed contentment. Her hand splayed across his chest, and she felt it rise and fall, felt his heart still hammering.

For long minutes of silence they held each other. He gently stroked the curve of her back while she swirled her fingers in lazy circles through the fine, tawny hair around his nipples. She felt soft and glowing and wonderful. She began to chuckle softly.

"Was it that funny?"

She felt him kiss her hair and snuggled in closer. "I was just thinking that this probably isn't what Roger meant when he told us to collaborate." She brushed her lips across his nipple and felt him shiver in response. In a voice ripe with insinuation, she murmured, "I want you to know . . . I'm ready to collaborate again."

When he didn't respond, Julia raised herself on one

elbow to look into his face. He gave her a sad, disturbing smile and tucked a stray curl behind her ear.

She felt a tremor of dismay. "What is it, Martin? What's the matter?"

"Julia, we need to talk and we can't do it like this."

He gently eased her from the crook of his arm, got up to his knees, and swiftly pulled his clothes back on. Without a word, he helped her into her jumpsuit, dressing her like a child. His actions were caring and loving, but they had a finality that made her uneasy. Something had changed.

For the first time in her life she'd come right out and asked a man to make love to her and he had very sweetly but definitely put her off. Her skill as a temptress must leave a lot to be desired. But deep inside she felt cold and uneasy.

Martin settled his back against the couch and pulled her against him, resting her head on his shoulder, rocking slightly back and forth and stroking a gentle hand up and down her back. "Are you all right?"

She nodded her head against his shoulder. "Yes," she whispered, "but I'm confused."

"Oh, Julia, you're so sweet and so honest and that's exactly why we have to put an end to this wonderful madness before it goes any farther."

"But maybe I don't want to." She could feel his heart thudding, his body tight and rigid.

"When you've had time to consider this, I think you'll be glad. It all happened too quickly. We got caught up in mutual desire and it's easy to forget about the things that are important to you. You just told me what you want from a relationship and I can't give you any of that. God knows I want you. You can't possibly be in any doubt now."

A shudder of desire raced through her to hear him say it out loud. She lifted her face to look at him.

"But I'll be moving on in a few months' time. If

you think you can handle an involvement on that basis, then I have to tell you that what I want more than anything right now is to take you upstairs and make love all night long. But that's not for you, is it, my dear?'' He held her gaze, his gentle tone bringing sudden tears to her eyes.

Julia shook her head. ''You're absolutely right, of course.'' She slowly pulled away from him, trying to smile, but it just resulted in a wistful trembling of her lips as he let her go. ''I'm glad you were in control enough to be sensible about this.''

''In control . . .'' He laughed humorlessly. ''If I didn't care about you and I wasn't concerned about hurting you, things would be very different right now.'' His eyes darkened as they held hers, intent and serious. ''Believe me, I don't take making love that lightly.'' His expression changed, and that wicked smile crept into his eyes. ''Besides, you'd never respect me again if I allowed myself to become your boy toy.''

She laughed weakly and her eyes brimmed over, tears spilling down her cheeks.

Carefully, tenderly, he wiped away the tears with his fingertips. ''That's better. I'd never forgive myself if I made you cry.''

Suddenly all the lights went out and they were left in darkness, sitting in the flickering glow of the fire.

''Damn!'' Martin stood up and reached for his sweater. ''The power line must be down.'' Julia slowly got to her feet as he pulled it on. ''Do you remember seeing any candles or a flashlight?''

She shook her head, still too bemused and shaken to cope immediately.

''We could be in big trouble.'' He made his way into the kitchen and she could hear him rummaging in the drawers.

''What do you mean?'' Julia followed, barely able

to make out his shadowy form in the darkened kitchen, far from the light of the fire.

"If we have no power, we have no heat. We'll freeze in our beds before morning." Martin slammed the last drawer shut with a muttered curse.

"At least we've got the fire. We could always bed down in front of it." She followed behind him to the living room again and cannoned into him when he stopped abruptly and turned to face her.

"Like I said before, we could be in big trouble."

In the flickering firelight she saw his grim expression and suddenly knew what he was thinking. There was only so much temptation any human being could stand. After the way passion had exploded between them, spending the night huddled together for warmth could have only one result.

Martin walked over to the door and pushed the curtain aside. "At least it's stopped snowing." He pulled his parka off the coat rack and put it on.

"What are you doing?"

"If we want to get out of here in the morning, I'd better dig my car out." His voice was muffled as he leaned down to pull on his boots.

"You could do that tomorrow." She came to stand beside him, and when he straightened up, he was very close to her, so close she had to crane her neck to look into his face.

He leaned toward her until she could feel his warm breath on her cheek. "I think that if I want to keep what's left of my virtue intact, I'd better do it now." With his lips barely an inch away from hers, he suddenly stepped back.

The heavily ironic inflection in his voice brought an unwilling smile to her face as she reached for her own coat.

"What are *you* doing?" Now it was his turn to sound surprised.

"I'm not staying here by myself. I'm coming with you."

"It's cold out there. You'll freeze," he objected.

"I don't care," she said flatly.

"You know, Julia, there's something I'm discovering about you. You're a very stubborn woman." He opened the door and stepped out.

The chill air on her face made Julia turn up her collar and pull her wool hat more snugly over her ears as she followed him, struck by the most momentous, obvious revelation.

Yes, and there's something I've discovered about me, too. I'm in love with you, Martin.

TEN

When had it happened? Julia stepped out onto the porch and blinked in the unexpected brightness of the full moon on the snow-covered landscape. When had she fallen in love with him?

She paused and took a deep breath of the cold air, pungent with wood smoke, and gazed in awe at a breathtaking scene. Under a clear dark sky, spangled with stars, the fields glittered, smooth and blue-white. The boughs of the dark fir trees sheltering the house to the north sagged under their heavy burden of snow, and the bare cluster of birches to the south shimmered like frosty jewels in the moonlight. A magical world, made to order for the wonder she felt inside. Her heart felt so full she could burst.

Martin had already left the porch. She followed his footsteps around the side of the house and met him coming back, carrying two snow shovels and an old corn broom.

"I found them in the shed. Here." He handed her a shovel and she swung it up onto her shoulder as he began trudging up the lane, the crunch of his footsteps resounding in the utter silence.

Barely giving a second glance to her nearly buried car, Julia followed in his tracks, her steps slow and awkward in the effort to match his longer stride, but it was easier than blazing her own trail. The snow had drifted knee-deep in some places.

She stopped for a moment to get her breath and watched Martin slogging on down the lane. How could it have happened, when until just a week ago they had treated each other with nothing but cold hostility? Yet, in spite of that, Julia knew she'd felt an awareness of him since the first day they met. She thought back to the many moments of shared anger and laughter. So much laughter. Had it happened in any of those moments? And why hadn't she noticed?

Martin stopped and turned to look at her. "Are you all right, Julia?"

"Yes . . . fine." She began walking again. Fine was an understatement. She felt so euphoric she could dance up the lane. Was this how love made you feel? This emotional roller coaster that had her wild with passion one minute and wanting to dance in the moonlight like a crazy fool the next.

No wonder it had seemed so right, lying in his arms, wanting to give herself completely. With Brian she'd held back, telling herself she was waiting for marriage. But she hadn't loved him. And making love was the ultimate closeness, something she wanted to share with the man she loved.

Near the end of the lane she caught up with Martin standing by a chest-high, snow-covered dome and knew that somewhere underneath his Honda had to be hiding.

The moonlight turned his fair hair to silver and deepened the shadows beneath his cheekbones as he grinned down at her. "Got any energy left for shoveling?"

She returned the smile, feeling their old playfulness begin to revive. "You're talking to a dyed-in-the-wool

Canadian here. Don't judge me by your wimpy English standards."

He rewarded her cheeky remark with a mittful of cold, wet snow in the face and Julia laughed as she brushed it away.

With the broom she swept off the car, then joined Martin as he labored to clear a path out to the road. Lifting shovelful after shovelful of heavy snow, she worked by his side in amicable silence. It had become quite mild in the aftermath of the storm, but even if it hadn't, the backbreaking work would have kept her warm.

Leaning on her shovel, she paused to catch her breath, watching Martin as he worked steadily on. Was he trying to wear himself out so that, when they finally returned to the darkened house, he wouldn't be capable of anything except falling into an exhausted sleep?

He paused to unzip his parka, then doggedly lifted another shovelful of snow. Four feet of laneway still remained to clear.

I've fallen in love with the wild man from Borneo, she smiled to herself. But she could never tell him. He didn't return her feelings, and she knew him well enough now to realize he'd feel guilty and responsible, because he was a wonderfully caring man.

Martin paused, breathing heavily, and tapped her on the shoulder, pointing toward the house. Through the bare trees she could see the yellow glow of lighted windows. The power had come back on.

"Why don't we leave the rest till morning. We'll have to wait until the road gets plowed anyway." He surveyed the uncovered Honda, sounding intensely relieved.

"It's been quite a while since I shoveled that much snow." Setting a steaming mug of hot chocolate in front of her, Martin sank down into the wooden chair at the old oak dining table. "Reminds me of the blizzard that hit Amblesey when I was twelve. I had to dig out a lot of half-frozen sheep that day, I can tell you."

Julia took a grateful sip and looked across at him, feeling the tender urge to lean over and push the tangle of damp hair off his forehead. He might be tired, sweaty, and in need of a shave, but right now he was just about the most beautiful man she'd ever seen. A secret sense of wonder filled her heart, just knowing now this was the man she loved. Julia hugged the secret tightly to herself, feeling happy and close to him in the strangest way, even though she couldn't share it.

"I wonder if that was the year *we* lived in England?" She sipped the sweet hot chocolate. "I remember there was a big storm that winter, but by spring we were off to Cyprus. After that it was Gibraltar and I didn't see snow again until Dad was stationed in Alberta." She smiled. "Of course, in two years there I got more than my fill of winter."

He smiled and his blue eyes held hers. He had wonderful eyes. Expressive and warm, filled with humor, eyes that made her want to pour out her innermost thoughts. Before long she found herself telling him more about her life as an army brat.

"My father was a military attaché. He was posted from one embassy to another throughout my childhood, dragging my mother and me around the world with him. Then when I was twelve I went away to boarding school."

He regarded her thoughtfully. "Was that difficult for you?"

"It wasn't the kind of life that suited me, but most of the other kids I met didn't seem to have trouble adjusting. Maybe it was because I was an only child, I don't know." She shrugged. "Time after time I'd make a really close friend, and then one of our fathers would be transferred and it would be all over. We'd write, of course, but that always dwindled away. And then the girls at the boarding school came from all over the world. Once we'd graduated, everyone scattered."

"It sounds like you had a pretty lonely time of it, Julia."

She looked down into her cup and sighed. "I took it badly every time. I never got used to it. And for a while, when I was younger, I blamed the major. I felt that if it weren't for him my mother and I could have settled down in that little house we used to love dreaming about."

She thought of her mother's comforting words whenever they were faced with yet another transfer. This wouldn't last forever. Someday they would settle down in one place and move into that little home of their own. Mom could have her rose garden, and Julia could finally have a stable life like normal children.

"But you never did."

"Well . . . finally Dad got posted to Ottawa. A long-term job with the Defense Department. They bought a place just outside the city. But by then I was seventeen. A year later I was off to college."

"That must have been better for you, given you a chance to make new 'permanent' friends." He swirled the hot chocolate at the bottom of his mug and drained his cup.

"Not really," she sighed. "By then I suppose the pattern had been set. I'd spent so much of my life shying away from close relationships and protecting myself from hurt that it had become a habit. I kept pretty much to myself and I suppose I got a reputation for being unsociable and aloof," she finished softly.

"You must have gotten over that then, because I couldn't help noticing how well liked you are at the magazine. I could see from the start that you had a pretty good rapport with just about everyone there . . . Everyone, that is, except one."

And she knew by his look who that exception had been. She laughed. "I can tell you it took a lot of practice and conscious effort to get over those feelings. Maybe journalism was the best job I could have chosen. As long as I have a reason for talking to someone I'm fine. But even now when I'm at big social functions, or I meet a new person, I'm scared to death of not knowing the right thing to say."

He leaned an elbow on the table and propped his chin on one hand, his face pensive. "Well, it certainly doesn't show. You know, you shouldn't be afraid of people. The way I feel is that every relationship enriches your life. As a writer, I find every relationship is grist for the mill, no matter how short it might be. People fascinate me. I want to know all I can about them, but you have to take the risk of opening yourself up to them in return."

She drank the last of her hot chocolate and put the mug down on the table. How she envied him that ability, but she knew she couldn't be so casual. She couldn't let go so easily. Friends were hard won for her, and when she made them, she wanted to keep them. And now she'd lost her heart to a man who would be out of her life in a few short months. And there was nothing she could do about it. Suddenly her happiness evaporated into something very like despair.

"I think I'll turn in now," she mumbled and rose to her feet. It would be so easy to walk around the table and sink down into his arms. Just let it all happen again. For as long as it lasted it would be heaven. But the pain of saying good-bye would be pure hell.

He stood up and walked her to the bottom of the stairs. She sensed the heavy, unspoken tension in him as he kept a careful distance between them. "Good night, Julia."

He sounded more quiet and sober than ever before and she could barely look at him. As she slowly climbed the stairs, she saw him pick up a book that had been lying on the end table and stretch out on the couch.

The cab driver handed Julia her change and looked dubiously in his rearview mirror at the snowy, rutted lane behind him. "Sure you'll be able to get out of here?"

"I'll be fine, thanks." To her surprise, her little red Escort was no longer buried under a mound of snow but sat in front of the farmhouse gleaming in the sunshine.

Amy had told her that Mr. McKinley from the neighboring farm would have the lane all plowed when she got there. But she hadn't expected him to clear her car, too. She'd have to call and thank him. He'd saved her at least half an hour of hard work.

She watched the cab jounce down the lane and took a breath of the mild air, enjoying the warmth in the last rays of the late afternoon sun. She had been impatient to retrieve Sarah Balfour's diary and couldn't wait a moment longer for Martin to get back and drive her out to get her car, as he had offered, so she'd called a cab instead.

Thinking about Martin brought a thrill of happiness mingled with despair. She hadn't seen him all day long, not since this morning.

She had woken from an incredibly erotic dream that Martin was making love to her, his hands, his mouth on her skin, bringing her to the brink of ecstacy. It had felt so intensely real, she could have cried out in frustration when she realized he wasn't in the bed beside her.

Underneath the warm quilt her naked body had throbbed with feverish desire. At that moment, more than anything else, she wanted to call out to him, to come and satisfy this need that made her body ache. One touch from him would be enough. Instead she jumped abruptly out of bed, shivering as the cold air hit her heated flesh.

As she quickly dressed, she glanced out the window to see a brilliant world of white. According to her watch, it was already ten-thirty. She'd slept surprisingly well, all things considered.

On her way downstairs she noticed one of the bunks in the larger room had obviously been slept in. Thank goodness she'd fallen asleep before she heard him come upstairs.

It was one thing to make a calm, rational decision that the attraction between them couldn't go any farther. But it was another thing entirely to ignore the fact that the man she loved and wanted so much was just in the next room.

When she got downstairs, she found Martin sitting at the dining room table, his feet propped on the opposite chair, a book in one hand and a mug of coffee in the other.

He looked up at her and smiled and her heart flipped over, even though it was the most casual of smiles. And that had set the tone for the rest of the morning. Neutral, friendly, but that was all.

After downing their coffee, they had tidied the kitchen and left. Martin had given her a lift to the George, then driven off again.

In all the rush she'd forgotten the diary and wanted to finish reading it. She wanted to know more about Sarah. Almost two hundred years had passed since Sarah had died, but in those pages the young girl seemed to come to life again. And that was what she wanted to do with her story. Bring all those people like Sarah back to life, make them real.

Julia stepped into the dim house and stared at the ashes in the fireplace with a sigh. It felt so cold and unwelcoming today. What a difference the presence of one man could make. Slipping off her snowy boots, she tried to shake her gloomy thoughts and padded toward the living room. Just get the diary and go.

It all happened so quickly she barely had time to register the figure wearing a black balaclava stepping out from behind the massive chimney and dashing toward the front door. Before she could react, a rough push sent her flying backward to slam her head against the abrasive stonework. For an instant of searing pain she thought her skull must have cracked like an egg. Then everything went black.

Martin wrenched the wheel savagely and the back end of the Honda slid out of control as he turned off the main highway onto the snow-covered dirt road. He was going too fast, but he didn't care.

He slammed his hand against the wheel. "Dammit! Why did she have to go out there?" He almost skidded off the road on an icy patch and swore viciously.

Why didn't she wait? Why did she have to be so bloody stubborn and independent? He had told her not to go out to the farmhouse. Why couldn't she listen to him? He felt like wringing her neck. A cold shiver went through him. But if she was dead, he'd never forgive himself.

As she struggled back to consciousness, Julia became aware of a dull, sickening throb, as if someone were taking a padded hammer to the back of her head. Her eyes slowly flickered open and focused on a white-painted baseboard a foot away. She was lying on her side, on the floor. But where?

Then it all came flooding back. She tried to get to her knees, but a wave of terrible nausea and dizziness washed over her, and she sank down again on the pine boards, terrified of getting sick or blacking out.

Oh God, what if he came back to hurt her? Her head throbbed in dull agony, and the sense of weak, helpless terror made her feel as vulnerable as a child. She wanted her mother. She began to cry and the tears rolled down her cheeks until she could taste the salt on her parted lips.

No, she had to stop this. Calm down. Gradually, by force of will, the tears stopped. After a few minutes the pain and sickening dizziness seemed to lessen and she was able to crawl across to the couch and sag against it, resting her head on the cool chintz seat cushion.

If she just stayed here for a while, maybe she'd be all right. She put a tentative hand to the back of her head and gingerly touched a lump the size of a small egg. She winced at the pain, but when she drew her hand away, she could see no sign of blood.

How long had she sat there? Still a little dazed and hardly daring to move her head, she heard the sound of running footsteps on the wooden porch outside and the front door burst open with a crash.

"Julia?"

She heard the sharp edge of fear in Martin's voice and lifted her head as he rushed into the room and saw her.

He reached her in two strides, threw himself down at her side, and took her into his arms. Profound relief swept over her. She clung to him helplessly, just wanting him to hold her, feeling the rapid rise and fall of his chest under the parka, his hard body trembling.

"Are you all right?" His voice was rough and urgent.

Julia nodded her head, then wished she hadn't, crying out as pain went knifing through her and the room gave a sickening lurch. She sank against his shoulder again, automatically putting a hand to the bump. He gently removed her fingers, and then she felt him parting the hair to examine her scalp.

"What happened?" he demanded.

In halting words she told him. ". . . but why are *you* here, Martin?" Maybe he wasn't here, turning up like her guardian angel. Maybe she was hallucinating.

"I got a call at the George. Someone obviously trying to disguise their voice, telling me that you were here and in trouble. Then they hung up. There was something very familiar about that voice. I can't put my finger on it, but it's driving me crazy." Beneath the anxiety Julia could still hear the anger that made his body taut. "Can you stand? I think we should have a doctor look at that bump."

"I'll try."

Hanging on to Martin, she got to her feet, and he put a supporting arm around her waist. They slowly headed for the door, but her head was spinning and her knees felt wobbly. She slumped gratefully against him.

"Oh, for God's sake!" He swept her up and carried her out to the Honda, installing her in the passenger seat.

"Martin, wait!" She clutched at his sleeve as he started to back away. "The diary."

He gave her a blank look.

"Could you get me Sarah's diary?"

He nodded and ran back into the house, returning a moment later with the small leather-bound volume and handed it to her as he slid into his seat and started the car. He'd barely said a word, yet Julia couldn't shake the feeling that he was angry. With her. But she couldn't wrestle with the reasons right now. Her head was throbbing unbearably. Closing her eyes, she leaned back against the seat.

At the small local hospital the intern in emergency ruled out a concussion, and Julia sighed with relief. He sent her off with a prescription for painkillers, warning her she might have a rotten headache for a few days.

At Martin's insistence, she filled the prescription, then ate a sandwich at the hospital cafeteria, feeling increasingly awkward under his stern gaze. It was nearly nine before they finally drove back to the George.

Although solicitous of her needs, he'd said practically nothing since coming to her rescue. Just looked at her, his face tightly set. The longer he stayed silent, the worse she felt.

As Martin stood by his door, waiting for her to go into her room, she knew she couldn't stand this tension a moment longer.

"Are you ever going to tell me what you're angry about? Or are you just going to give me the silent treatment for the rest of my life?"

His jaw tightened. "I don't think this is a good time to discuss it. We'll talk tomorrow morning after you've had a good night's sleep."

"If you think I'm going to get a good night's sleep with this hanging over my head, you're crazy." Julia swallowed hard. She felt like bursting into tears.

In reply he opened his door, ushering her inside and closing it behind him. Still shaky, she sank down onto the brass bed, as it occurred to her that she'd never been in his room before. The layout mirrored her own, but her gaze fell on his personal belongings. His red sweater neatly folded on top of the maple dresser, the velour bathrobe slung carelessly over the end of the bed.

Martin threw off his coat, taking a seat on the windowsill. She found it impossible to look at his cold, rigid face.

"Why are you so angry with me, Martin?" she asked quietly, keeping her eyes trained on the white chenille bedspread as her fingers picked compulsively at the tufts.

"I kept warning you, but you wouldn't pay any attention and you almost got yourself killed. I told you

I'd drive you out there. Why couldn't you have waited for me?''

He hadn't used that harsh, angry tone with her since they started work on this article, but now it upset her far more than it ever did before.

''I'm sorry, you're right. I should have waited. But how was I supposed to know something like this would happen?''

His lips compressed with impatience. Then he went on in a quieter voice. ''I've asked you this before, but now you're going to tell me. What are you working on, Julia?''

Torn, she hesitated for a moment. If she thought there was the faintest connection, she'd tell him everything right now. But lonely farmhouses got broken into all the time.

''I can't tell you yet, but believe me, it's nothing that could make anyone resort to violence.''

''You still don't trust me. Is that what it is?''

Beneath his quiet, matter-of-fact voice, she sensed the hurt. *Oh, Martin, if only you knew how I feel about you.*

''Of course I trust you.'' She leaned toward him earnestly, pleading with her eyes for him to understand. ''But you of all people should respect my right to keep this story to myself.''

He rose from the sill and sat down on the bed beside her, taking her hands in his lean, strong fingers, his denim-clad knee brushing hers. ''Look, Julia, don't you realize I feel responsible for you? I'm the one who suggested this stupid contest.''

She squeezed his hands, holding his gaze. ''And I'm glad you did. It's given me a chance to prove to myself what I'm capable of.''

Although the anger seemed to have dissipated, his face still had a steely set. ''Nevertheless, if we were working together, you wouldn't be facing this danger alone."

"Don't worry about me, Martin. I've got to learn to handle whatever comes along with the job. After all, you've faced far worse than this. You've been in war zones and nobody was holding your hand." Her gaze fell to their clasped hands.

"That's different." He dropped her hands and stood up, pacing over to the window to stare out into the darkness.

She followed his lithe movements with her eyes. "Why? Because you're a man and I'm a woman?"

He gave an impatient groan and swung around to face her. "Oh, don't start on that. You know it's got nothing to do with that at all."

"Then what does it have to do with?" she asked softly.

Martin turned to the window again. Julia rose and went to stand beside him. He seemed so disturbed, she felt the strangest need to comfort and reassure him.

"Look, I admit you're right. Heaven knows what this is all about, but from now on, I'll be more careful. Will that satisfy you?"

He looked down at her, his blue eyes dark and sober, then heaved a massive sigh. "Just promise me one thing. Don't go anywhere alone from now on."

"I promise." She held his grave look for a moment. "Now I think I'm going to bed." It was time for another painkiller. Her head was really beginning to throb.

As she turned to leave, Martin reached out and stopped her with a hand on her shoulder. When she looked up at him, questioning, he leaned down and touched her lips in a soft, gentle kiss.

ELEVEN

The note lay under her car keys on the dresser. On her way to the shower, Julia noticed the sheet of paper and picked it up.

Hope you don't mind my coming into your room for your keys, but you were fast asleep and I didn't want to wake you, she read. *I hope the return of your car will compensate for my taking such a liberty.*

She didn't need to see *Martin* scrawled assertively below to know who had written it. Then she read the P.S. "You look so adorable when you're asleep. It was hard to resist the urge to kiss you."

A strange little shiver passed through her and her lips curved in a small smile as she carefully folded the sheet of paper and stowed it in an inner pocket of her wallet. So did he resist, or had he kissed her? It was maddening not knowing.

It must have been a combination of fatigue and the painkillers, but she'd slept like a log, not waking until nearly eleven. After a quick shower, she slipped into black stirrup pants and a long, cozy teal sweater, then hurried downstairs to the kitchen.

"Morning, Amy." She found the innkeeper busy

chopping celery at the long pine table. "I was wondering if I could just get myself something to eat . . ."

"Well, my dear, of course!" Amy dropped her knife beside the cutting board and headed toward the large refrigerator. "I think some bacon and eggs are what you need." She pulled out a box of eggs, then took out a skillet.

Before Julia could open her mouth to object that she only wanted some toast and tea, Amy had settled her at the table and wouldn't let her say no to a full breakfast.

"You could use a bit more meat on your bones." She set a brimming glass of orange juice in front of her.

Julia obediently drank her juice. "Have you seen anything of Martin?" She tried to sound casual, but her thoughts kept returning to the disturbing intimacy of his watching her while she slept.

"He went off bright and early this morning." Amy drained the sizzling bacon and slid it onto Julia's plate. "Goodness knows where. That young man has boundless energy."

Swallowing the last mouthful of bacon and eggs, she felt revived and human again. Despite the doctor's prediction, her head didn't seem to be throbbing this morning. In fact, the only reminder of yesterday's frightening encounter at the farm was the lump on her head. It still hurt to touch, as she'd discovered when brushing her hair.

She had barely turned the brass handle and opened the white door of the *Gleaner* offices when an agitated Trudi came rushing out, clutching a tissue to her face.

What's wrong?" Julia gasped.

The other woman's reddened eyes darted back to Eric, standing in the center of the room behind her, before turning her tear-streaked face back to Julia.

"Julia, I . . ." she began.

"Trudi!" Eric's stern voice cut in. Shaking her head, she brushed past with a choking sob.

Watching her rush down the street, Julia bit her lip in concern. How she hated to see things going so badly between them. There was something very endearing about Trudi's open, artless friendliness. She'd grown to like her and feel a sense of sympathy for her situation. Especially now, loving Martin and knowing how hopeless it was. Couldn't Eric see that the reason Trudi went to such ridiculous lengths to make him jealous was because she was tired of waiting?

"I'll be right with you."

Sounding tense and edgy, Eric avoided Julia's eyes as he picked up maps and papers from the desk and shoved them into the deep pockets of his navy coat. He pulled on his cap and turned up the ear flaps, then smiled at her nervously.

"Shall we go?"

With a silent nod, she led the way out to her Escort parked at the curb.

Eric's call about finding the location of Titus Flynn's house had left her excited and glad to accept his offer to show her the spot. If her hunch was right, she could tie everything together. The smuggler mentioned in all the stories had undoubtedly been Titus Flynn, she had told him, and now she knew exactly what had happened to the paywagon.

As they drove out of town, skirting the wooden palisades of Fort George, Eric slumped down quietly in the seat.

"Just take the Niagara Parkway. I'll tell you when we get there."

He looked upset and preoccupied, and Julia felt a little guilty for dragging him away from his problems with Trudi. Heaven knows what had preceded the embarrassing scene she'd walked in on, but she could empathize with the insecurities he tried so hard to mask with his slightly pompous air. Unfortunately, making him jealous was probably the worst tactic Trudi could have chosen to get a commitment out of him.

Of course, she couldn't say that to either of them, and who was she to play amateur psychologist? She should be dealing with her own tangled emotions before poking her nose into other people's affairs.

Under a dull gray sky, the road wound between stands of bare trees, hugging the river a stone's throw away on their left. Up ahead, vivid orange against the snow, Julia noticed the tarpaulins covering the dig site. Now the archaeologists had finished, she wondered whether the Niagara Parks Commission would go ahead with the picnic shelter they had planned for the spot. She'd better give them a call.

Suddenly Eric straightened up. "It's just up ahead," he said, tracing a forefinger along the ordnance survey map on his lap.

With a tingle of elation, she pulled into the next rest area. This was it. She'd done it! Her theory was confirmed.

Jumping out of the car into the cold air, she trudged through the snow toward the river, in the direction Eric pointed, surveying the flat expanse of ground between the road and the trees edging the bank of the broad, majestic Niagara. Over to her left she could see the orange tarpaulin covering the site of the archaeological find.

The conspirators murdered by Oakshott had been two British officers, two Americans, and a civilian, shot down near Titus Flynn's farmhouse, which would have stood on this very spot, only a few hundred feet from where those remains had been found.

Julia felt like crowing with satisfaction and pride. She'd proved to herself that she could nose out a story and follow through, no matter what, that she really did have the instincts to be a good journalist.

She could hardly wait to write up the article and see the look on Martin's face. And suddenly she realized that she wanted him to be proud of her.

"Okay, Julia. I think it's time you told me the rest." Behind her Eric's voice had changed, hardened with a foreign note of aggressive determination.

She turned, bewildered, to see him gripping an old dueling pistol with two trembling hands. Hadn't she seen that behind a glass case in the museum?

She burst out laughing. "Oh come on, Eric. Is this some sort of a joke?"

"This is no joke, Julia." Indignant, his face went beet red. "You know where it is, don't you? And you're going to tell me. If you think I'm going to stand by and watch you walk away with that silver, after I've spent the last year looking for it, you can think again."

"The silver? What are you talking about?" She took a step toward him, but he backed away from her and Julia stopped. "There's no silver. It was taken a long time ago, Eric."

His pale eyes blinked rapidly beneath the woolen cap. "It's you and that friend of yours. You have plans to take it. Well, Trudi won't even look twice at him when I get what's rightfully mine," he said with vengeful petulance.

He waved the pistol menacingly and she felt an instant of real fear, wondering if it might be loaded after all. She couldn't even tell if there was a safety, or just how easily it might go off.

But hang on a minute. She reined in her thoughts as common sense took hold again. After all, this was Eric! And right now he looked scared to death. He might be deluded, but nothing could ever convince her that he'd be capable of hurting anybody.

"D . . . down there," he stammered, pointing toward the river with the pistol, his hand trembling pitifully. "You're going to show me where it is."

"Down there?" She looked down the steep wooded bank to the dark, ice-edged water. "You're crazy, that's dangerous."

"Well *I'm* dangerous, so you'd better do what I tell you."

He looked so frightened and the situation seemed so ludicrous, she felt an insane urge to laugh again.

Her glance fell to the traces of corrosion around the barrel of the silver-trimmed pistol. The only prospect really worrying her was that he might set the thing off accidentally and have it explode in his face. She decided to stall.

She peered cautiously over the edge. "What do you imagine is down there?"

His eyes darted rapidly from the steep incline back to her face. "You supplied me with the missing link in my investigation. Titus Flynn."

Of course. He'd only know about Titus Flynn if he'd been able to read Sarah's diary. And thanks to Uncle Harry he never got a chance.

"I went back through all the records and anecdotal accounts," he continued, "and I discovered one of the more interesting rumors around the town before the war. People believed he had a tunnel system from the water's edge to his house to conceal his smuggled goods." His voice had become more high pitched and shaky. He sounded close to tears. "But, of course, you know that, don't you. Because that's where the silver is, isn't it?"

"But, Eric, when I said I knew what had become of the silver, I meant I knew who had taken it," Julia explained patiently, trying to keep her voice even and matter-of-fact, hoping she could calm him enough to listen to reason. "Those men were murdered by a British officer who took the silver and disappeared. Don't you understand? That's the important part. Those remains aren't just anonymous bodies anymore. I know now what they were doing there."

"I . . . I don't believe you." His face paled under the freckles except for the vivid splotches of red on his cheeks. "You're just trying to mislead me. Then you'll come back later and get it for yourself."

Julia could see doubt creeping into his eyes. Beginning to feel optimistic, she pressed her advantage. "Don't you see, Eric. There is no silver." She reached out a comforting hand. "Now why don't we just go on back to the car and . . ."

"No!" He waved the pistol wildly. "We're going down there. Now."

Julia dropped her hand. How was she going to bring him to his senses? He looked more frightened than she felt. She stood up a little straighter and put a note of authority into her voice. She wasn't Major Bennett's daughter for nothing.

"This is ridiculous. Now put that thing down. You might hurt somebody." Eric flinched, lowering the pistol a little, and Julia felt encouraged. "We'll go back to town and I'll show you what I found out. Maybe that will convince you."

From behind came the sound of a car tearing around the curve at high speed, and she turned to see Martin's battered Honda pull up to a screaming halt beside her car a hundred yards away.

A muffled exclamation of terror, then a scream, made her jerk around just in time to see Eric tumbling down the snowy slope amid the snapping of breaking branches. In horror she watched him slide over the shelf of ice edging the river and disappear under the dark, rushing water.

Without a second thought, Julia launched herself down the slope after him, hanging on to tree trunks and the bare, spindly sumac branches to keep herself from sliding in, too. Over the sound of the river she could hear Martin shouting her name in the distance, but she didn't have time to answer him.

Eric surfaced, flailing, and grabbed at an overhanging branch with one hand. His cap had gone and he was sobbing and gasping as Julia reached the bottom of the slope. In the frigid, fast moving water, with the weight of his heavy coat pulling him down, she knew he wouldn't be able to hold on for long.

Going by instinct, she dropped onto her stomach, inching her way across the narrow shelf of ridged ice edging the river until she could grab his wrist with both hands. Hanging on with all her strength, she could feel the powerful current tugging at him.

"I can't feel the bottom!" His eyes blazed with terror.

She tried to sound strong and reassuring. "It's all right. I won't let you go." If he panicked, she might not be able to hold him. Julia pulled harder as Eric made frantic attempts to scramble up onto the ice shelf, but it kept breaking away under his weight.

"Martin!" she screamed, feeling herself sliding closer to the edge, her hands so numb she couldn't feel Eric's wrist and knew she couldn't hold on much longer.

Then she heard branches breaking, the sound of Martin scrambling down the steep riverbank. A hand appeared over her shoulder, grabbed Eric's arm, and began to pull. Together, they dragged him out of the water, to lie panting, coughing, and shivering on a mound of snow at the base of the slope.

Martin pulled her roughly to her feet and turned her to face him. "Are you all right? I swear if he's hurt you I'll throw him back in the river myself." He gripped her arms so tightly, he almost cut off her circulation.

"I'm fine," she gasped, clinging to him gratefully for a moment, before the sound of Eric's sobbing brought her over to him, still huddled on the ground. She pulled off his sodden wool coat and went to remove her own to cover him. Martin stopped her and unzipped his parka, his face grim and tight with anger.

"You're the one responsible for all the break-ins and that phone call yesterday, aren't you?"

His voice sounded colder than the icy river as he yanked Eric upright and helped him, shivering and in shock, into the warm parka.

"I'm sorry, I'm sorry." Eric turned beseeching eyes to Julia and sobbed. "I tried to put you off the story, but you kept going after it. I even tried to frighten you when I got into your room . . ."

"That uniform . . ." she murmured.

"Yes." He nodded and pressed his lips together. "From the museum . . . But that didn't work. I should have known. I never meant to hurt you, any of those times. Then yesterday, I was so afraid I'd killed you, that's why I made that phone call." He held a shaky hand out in a pleading gesture, then drew it back. "Please believe me, I never meant to hurt you. That gun wasn't even loaded. I just wanted the information. I had to get it first." He broke down and began to weep.

Julia stepped closer and put her arm around him. "Come on, Eric, we've got to get you to a hospital, to somewhere warm." She started trying to move him up the slope. "It's all right. It's all over now. I know you meant me no harm. I understand, I really do."

He was obviously in a state of shock and didn't respond to her urging. She turned and looked at Martin behind her. With an impatient tightening of his lips, he moved closer and took Eric's other arm. It was painfully clear that Eric's pitiful explanations hadn't softened his anger.

Oblivious to their attempts to help him, Eric hung back, clutching at Julia with cold, desperate fingers.

Obviously nothing she'd said had penetrated. "I don't expect you to understand, but I had to make something of myself for Trudi. I *had* to. Otherwise I'd lose her. And now we're finished."

Laboring up the slope, Julia stumbled over a root and almost fell but for Eric's unexpected steadiness. Thank goodness he wasn't as weakened by his experience as she'd feared.

"You're wrong, you know," she gasped, short of breath from climbing the steep, rough ground. "I think you should talk to her. I'm sure you two can work out your problems, but you have to talk about it."

She glanced over and caught Martin's look of disgusted pity as he continued helping Eric up the slope, his face set, his eyes trained on the rough ground ahead. Voices sounded from above and they all looked up to see two mounties peering over the bank.

"The patrol helicopter said someone was in the river." The first officer cast an assessing look at Eric, his red hair still lank and clinging to his skull. "Anybody else go in?" He peered down toward the dark water and Julia shivered to think how close she had come.

"No one else, but thank God you're here, Officer. My friend here lost his footing and fell. It could have been a real tragedy if Mr. Taylor hadn't been here to help." She turned meaningful eyes toward Martin.

Although he didn't contradict her, she could tell from the twist of his lips that he was far from pleased at her withholding the real story from the police. But she just couldn't bring herself to turn Eric in. After all, she was safe and Eric looked so pathetic.

As the officers leaned over to help Eric over the lip of the bank, she saw the numb, defeated look in his eyes and knew that any anger she might have felt against him had long since gone.

When they gained the top, one officer began leading Eric toward the waiting cruiser, while the other opened his notebook and turned to Julia, pencil poised. "May I ask what you were doing down here, please?"

Hunched in the borrowed parka, Eric paused and looked back over his shoulder toward her with misery in his eyes, resigned to his fate.

"I'm a journalist." Julia shoved her icy hands into her coat sleeves for warmth. "I'm working on a story about the archaeological dig just up the road and I was scouting out the area. Eric was helping me when he fell in."

"You're very lucky, sir, not to have been swept away." The officer shook his head at Eric, who stared at Julia in dazed disbelief. She shot him an encouraging smile. "Now," the policeman continued, "we'd better get you to the hospital."

Standing by her Escort, Julia turned to Martin as the officers bundled Eric into the car and pulled away. "Thank God you came, but how on earth did you turn up here?"

"Trudi hauled me in off the street and started babbling that Eric had gone mad." His voice was strained. "She finally told me what he planned to do, but only after I promised I wouldn't hurt him. I can tell you I felt ready to commit murder when she said she was afraid you were in trouble."

Julia looked away from the anger and concern in his eyes and rubbed her arms. So Eric had told Trudi. That's why she'd been so upset at his office. Now that it was all over and her adrenalin had slowed down, Julia felt exhausted and cold.

Martin's tone softened. "Listen, you're freezing. It's mad to be having a conversation here. Let's get back to the George. We'll talk there."

* * *

Amy picked up the tray off the quilt covering Julia's knees. "I'm glad you ate up all that soup. Now I want you to stay right there in that bed until tomorrow."

From the minute they had walked into the George and Amy saw Julia's pale face and damp, disheveled appearance and heard the story of Eric's mishap, she had taken over like a bustling mother hen. After bundling Julia into a hot bath, she had given her strict orders to get to bed. And Julia just felt too tired and emotionally strung out to argue.

As soon as Amy left with the tray, she got up, padded barefoot over to the dresser for her hairbrush, and sat back down again on the side of her bed. Pulling off the elastic, she unbraided her hair, then shook out the wavy auburn strands with a sigh.

She wanted to see Martin, but Amy told her she'd banished him from her room. After all, her patient needed her rest. The innkeeper's motherly concern made Julia impatient and restive, but she couldn't be so ungrateful as to argue.

A light tapping at the window made her look up to see a welcome face on the other side of the glass. She rushed over, unlocked the window, and dragged up the sash. Martin crawled in.

"What are you doing?" She found herself whispering, half expecting Amy to be listening at the door.

"I wanted to talk to you."

He closed the window, sat on the sill, and folded his arms, his gaze sliding over her with a deceptively lazy expression that made her all too aware of being in her blue flannel pajamas.

"Why didn't you use the door? Or is that too conventional for you?"

A sudden breathless excitement made her legs feel weak as she returned to the bed and resumed brushing her hair with hands that had begun to tremble.

"Because Amy the Gorgon is just down the hall as

we speak. She stood there folding laundry and threatening me within an inch of my life if I disturbed you tonight. Or subjected you to 'any more of my nonsense' as she put it." He raised his eyebrows with a devilish grin. "What do you suppose she meant by that?"

"Amy's no fool. She's got your number." Julia gave a tremulous laugh and began struggling with a large tangle in her hair. She wished he would stop watching her. He was making her very nervous. "So what did you want to talk to me about?"

He came over to the bed, taking the brush from her inept, suddenly nerveless fingers, and stood beside her as he began untangling the knot. Her glance slid to his narrow jean-clad hips, level with her eyes, then darted away again. His gentle hands lingered in her hair a moment too long, and her heart skittered with mingled joy and trepidation.

"What the hell was that all about today?" he said quietly. "I know you were on the trail of something that obsessed Eric enough he'd go to those absurd lengths. Trudi babbled on about hidden silver, but frankly I didn't pay much attention. I was more worried about that maniac hurting you."

He sat down behind her, the soft old mattress gave beneath his weight, and she could feel his thigh grazing the curve of her hip. Julia closed her eyes at the sensations racing through her.

"You were that concerned about me?" she croaked, then quickly cleared her throat.

"You idiot, of course I was concerned."

This tender speech helped distract her a little from the feeling of his warm fingers on the back of her neck, the slow, soothing way he stroked the brush through her hair as he continued.

"So are you going to tell me what on earth you've been working on?"

Julia smiled impishly. "You'll just have to wait for the May cover story."

"God, you're a stubborn woman. I see I'll have to set an example and show you that I trust you, even if you don't trust me."

His long-suffering tone made her laugh. "No . . . please. I don't want to know. Let's stick to the terms of the contest, submit the stories anonymously, and wait for Roger's verdict."

How the world had turned upside down in one short week. Now she wanted to win more than ever. Not to score points off Martin, but because, in some crazy way, she wanted him to feel proud of her for sticking to the deal and showing him what she could do.

And he wouldn't be a bad loser. He might be competitive, but, for all his blithe dismissal of convention, he had an ingrained sense of honor. How wrong she had been about him. Julia sat a little away and turned to Martin, suddenly serious.

He shrugged. "Okay, we'll see it through to the bitter end. And after that . . ." His voice trailed off as he met her eyes.

Vibrant awareness seemed to shimmer in the air between them. Looking into his lean, handsome face, Julia felt suddenly overcome with such an intense rush of love for him, her eyes filled with tears.

A small frown creased his brow, a wondering, concerned look. Cupping her chin gently in his hand, he drew her forward and his mouth melted against hers in a soft, warm kiss, tender and comforting. Pure need trembled through her and her lips softly parted. Shy and tentative, she slowly ran the tip of her tongue along the line of his lips.

He stilled for a moment with a sharp, quick intake of breath. Then his strong arms went around her and pulled her close, almost crushing her against him. His mouth opened on hers with a desperation that made her senses reel, as if he'd been needing her forever and couldn't wait another second to finally possess her.

Julia melted into him, her mouth as hungry and seeking as his. He tilted his head to deepen the kiss and slowly lowered her down onto the bed. Through her flannel pajamas she could feel the coolness of the quilt on her heated skin, the warmth and weight of his body partly covering her own.

He lay on his side, leaning over her, one leg drawn up to rest heavily across her hips. Urgent, demanding, his kisses inflamed her, then slowed, became maddeningly teasing, his tongue grazing, caressing. She tangled her fingers in his silky hair, trailed them over the smooth planes of his face.

Through the soft flannel she could feel his hand, resting on her waist, slide over her ribs to curve under the swell of her breast. Warm liquid heat filled her blood and a little moan came from her throat as she shifted her hips, straining against his thigh.

With a soft groan he pulled her closer to the warmth of his body, until she could feel the hard arousing pressure she craved.

A knock sounded at the door. "Julia? Julia dear?"

At the sound of Amy's voice Martin leapt off her as if she were made of hot coals. Julia jerked upright in total confusion, then choked back a giggle at the hunted look on Martin's face. As if Amy held more terror for him than facing a whole battalion of South American guerrillas.

"Sorry to disturb you," her voice floated through the panels of the door, "but I thought you might like something to keep you warm and cozy in bed."

Julia stared wide-eyed at Martin, then clapped a hand to her mouth, trying to stifle her laughter at the knowing, wicked amusement now filling his eyes.

"Uh . . . Just a minute," she stammered as he held

a cautioning finger to his lips, then walked softly over to station himself behind the door.

She approached on shaky legs and opened it a crack. Amy stood on the threshold with a bright smile and a blue hot-water bottle. Julia could feel her cheeks burning. It was absurd to feel so guilty. They hadn't been doing anything wrong and, anyway, they were both adults.

"Now just tuck this in by your feet, dear. We don't want you developing pneumonia, do we?"

Julia took the hot-water bottle with a grateful smile, burningly conscious of Martin standing behind the door, watching her intently, with a promise in his eyes that made her shiver with anticipation.

"Why, you're cold, child!" Amy's face creased with concern. "Now just you get into bed and I'll see you in the morning."

Julia closed the door, clutching the hot-water bottle to her chest as she stared at Martin. He reached out a hand and turned the lock, then began advancing toward her with a slow, deliberate tread.

With a quiver of excitement, she backed away from the wicked look in his eyes, until she felt the edge of the bed behind her trembling knees. Coming very close, he took the hot-water bottle gently from her hands. His eyes never left her face as he walked over to the window, pulled up the sash, and tossed the hot-water bottle out onto the veranda.

"You won't be needing that tonight." He closed the window and came purposefully toward her. Lowering her to the sheets, he murmured, "Now, where were we?"

She strained upwards to capture his mouth in a soft mingling of lips and tongues. This was insane, after deciding so logically not to do this again, but to hell with logic. She loved him, she was on fire with wanting him, and she had to take this chance. Julia sighed and twined her arms even tighter around his neck, pulling him down to lie against her.

"Wait a minute. Let's do this properly." Every part of him ached to have her, but he wanted to savor every moment. He pulled her up to a sitting position and began slowly unbuttoning her pajama top, teasing himself with the anticipation. "I must say I like your taste in pajamas, but I *love* your taste in lingerie." A sudden inspiration made him smile. "Maybe later you can put some on, so I can take it off you."

He slid his hands beneath the flannel to curve over her bare shoulders and felt her breathing quicken as he pushed off the pajama top, leaving her naked to the waist. With a quick intake of breath, he reached out to cup one perfect rounded breast in his hand, the small pink nipple tightening into a succulent little bud in response to the teasing brush of his thumb. Oh God, how could he ever have enough of her to slake his desire?

Julia blushed and glanced down at herself. "I . . . I'm not exactly overendowed."

She saw his blue eyes darken to cobalt, with a hazy, sensual amusement as he bent his head to her breast.

"Who cares . . ." he murmured distractedly. With a shuddery sigh Julia lay back, giving herself over completely to the feeling of his tongue caressing, the infinite sensations of pleasure shivering through every pore.

She felt his hands so strong, yet delicate in their touch, trailing over her skin like silk. He made a path of soft, wet kisses down to her navel, scarcely pausing to slide off her pajama bottoms. His mouth brushed over her belly and down to the juncture of her thighs. Her eyes flew open as she felt him move away.

"Don't stop," she gasped, her heart racing. But he had stood up and was pulling off his shirt, then began unbuckling his belt while his eyes never left her face.

"I couldn't if I tried." His voice dropped to a husky whisper as she watched him remove his clothes with a thrill of pure desire, the urgent need to reach out and touch. She wanted to press her lips to every lean, hard inch of his beautiful masculine body.

He lay down beside her and pulled her against him, mouths melting together in heady intimacy. She ran her hands over him in wonder, feeling the smooth play of muscle under skin, the dazzling pleasure of every slight friction of bare skin against bare skin. Hands gliding down his back, curving featherlight and tantalizing over sculpted muscular curves and hollows, then gently squeezing and stroking his smooth, warm flesh. Thigh brushing thigh, then intertwining with a pure erotic thrill, rough against smooth. *Touch me, just touch me . . .*

Drunk with pleasure, wanting it to go on forever, she could feel his erection pressing hard against her belly and suddenly knew that she needed him now. Right now. The warm, wanting ache between her thighs made her wriggle upwards, craving to be soothed, moving her hips against his, until she could feel him begin to enter her.

He pulled away with a groan. "Not yet, darling, not yet."

The sight of her lips softly parted, waiting to be kissed, made him want to crush her close, take her now. He had to slow down. Savor each wonderful sensation. The delicate perfume of her soft skin, the curve of her breast against his cheek, the tantalizing mixture of shyness and wanton need with which she gave a pleading moan and arched her body, turning so that her taut nipple brushed the corner of his mouth.

He took it gently, tracing the aureole in slow circles with his tongue, a leisured suckling that made her moan and writhe beneath him and drove him to the brink. He traced the inside of her slender thigh, her skin like silk, until he reached her softness, her silken flesh warm and wet for him.

She felt him moving lower, one hand sliding beneath

to curve her hips closer, the other gently parting her thighs. Her eyes fluttered open and she gazed down at his blond head, feeling his hair brushing like silk over her belly, the warmth of his mouth kissing her skin. She felt a rush of love for him so sweet and painful it pierced her to the heart. And a need that transcended physical desire.

"Julia . . . Julia . . ." She felt him whisper her name against her skin. ". . . you're so sweet . . ."

Then his mouth found her and her body exploded in an incandescent torrent of sensation. With a convulsive gasp, she arched and clutched at the bed sheets in melting, relentless delirium.

At her inarticulate cries of pleasure he couldn't hold back a second longer. He surged upwards, blind and urgent, wanting to drive into her so deeply they could never be separated. He'd never needed a woman like this before, wanted to lose himself in her.

She wrapped her long beautiful legs around his waist and urged him into her with soft pleading words, and every shred of reason fled. He found her mouth as she moved in frantic rhythm with him. Her luscious mouth, as hot and sweet as the cradle of soft curls clutching him so tightly.

Nothing existed but the blind, primitive ecstasy of taking her completely, making her his. Release ripped through him in racking shudders as Julia sobbed out his name against his mouth. Finally he slumped against her, gasping for breath, and gathered her close to him. He didn't think he could ever get her close enough.

Julia slowly woke up, conscious of a slight delicious ache between her thighs and a wonderful languid feeling in her limbs from a night spent making love.

She stretched with a smug contentment and smiled as she turned her head. The bed was empty. Except for the indentation of Martin's head on the pillow it might all have been an erotic dream.

She felt a tremor of dismay. Then she saw the note on the bedside table and a cold, ominous feeling made her heart beat uncomfortably in her throat. With trembling fingers she picked up the folded piece of paper and read the hastily scribbled words.

Julia, didn't want to wake you. Got an early call from Roger to fly out to the West Coast. See you in a few days. Love, Martin.

She could only stare at it blankly for a long moment and even glanced at the other side before it finally sank in. He had gone. And all he had left behind was an impersonal note to say good-bye. After what they had shared together, how could he?

Sinking down onto the pillows, she pulled up the quilt, torn with confusion. What if she'd misinterpreted his feelings last night, read too much into the way he seemed to care about her? His desire had been as urgent and powerful as her own. But that didn't mean he loved her.

She bit her lip and turned to stare out the window. What was she going to do? She wanted to be in his arms right now, needed him with an intensity that made her ache inside. But he obviously didn't feel the same way, not if he could leave her with only a casual, indifferent little note telling her when to expect him back. And when he returned, what then?

What had happened to her? For so long she'd guarded her emotions, carefully maintaining control over her life, protecting herself from hurt. If you lost control, the enemy had you, the major used to say.

Julia burrowed deeper into the pillow with a bitter smile. All those military axioms were the best way a taciturn but loving father had for giving advice about life. But they were of no use to her now.

All her defenses had melted away. She had walked

into the enemy camp and surrendered her heart, left herself naked and vulnerable. And when he was gone . . . she would suffer more deeply than she had ever suffered before.

And it had already begun—this tearing pain inside her heart, knowing that no matter what happened between them, one day he would be gone for good. Her throat tightened and she clutched at the quilt, helpless to stop the sudden feeling of despair from overwhelming her. No act of will could stop her from hurting.

Tears spilled out over her cheeks and a sob tore through her. She buried her head in the pillow, suddenly overcome, until her whole body shook with the intensity of her weeping.

TWELVE

"Both of these articles are good. It'll be a tough call. Although I have to admit it was a clever twist to use the ghost story. But dammit," Roger growled in irritation as he waved both articles at Julia across his desk, "I told you two to work together! You've got to get over your little problems."

Easier said than done, especially the little problem of falling in love with the wrong man. Julia slumped back in the chair.

"Don't worry about it, Roger. We've settled all that."

"Good, because this piece on native land claims shouldn't take Martin more than a week, and when he gets back from the West Coast, I'm thinking of having you really collaborate on another article. There's a story brewing in Labrador I might send you out on together."

The thought made her heart leap with a million contradictory impulses. In the five days since coming back to Toronto she hardly knew her own emotions from one moment to the next.

"Can't he handle it by himself?"

Roger's bulldog face furrowed with displeasure. "I

thought you said you'd solved your problems . . ." He broke off at the buzz of the intercom and picked up his phone.

Julia's gaze fell to her hands, making compulsive folds in her soft amethyst challis skirt. *You fool, you know you want to go. And you know what will happen if you're isolated with him again.*

When she'd woken the next morning at the George to find Martin gone, leaving only that casual note of explanation, she'd felt crushed and humiliated by her own hopes. It wasn't until she got back to the office on Monday morning, after a miserable weekend at home, that she'd learned Roger had sent him to the Pacific Northwest islands.

She still felt furious with herself for reacting like a deserted woman. He didn't have to explain himself to her, and he obviously didn't feel any need to. He was a free spirit with no ties, exactly as he wanted. This was what life with Martin would be like.

The thought brought her up short. There was no question about a life with Martin. But what did he expect of her? To be there every time he breezed into town, to be casual lovers with no commitment or expectations? That kind of relationship would make her miserable.

Roger put down the phone. "Look, we'll talk about this next week, when he gets back."

Taking her cue, Julia left his office, slipping past the secretary's desk, and headed for her cubicle.

Part of her dreaded Martin's return, afraid of the sharp eyes and knowing glances that would greet their newfound friendship. It would be impossible to hide her change of attitude from someone like Eunice, and Julia was afraid the atmosphere between Martin and herself would be interpreted all too accurately.

Yet in spite of her cautious instincts, she couldn't

wait for the day he sailed back in. She missed him. Life seemed drab and colorless without him.

She sank down into her chair and switched on her computer. Keep busy, that was all she could do. The office hum had changed key, and she could hear drawers closing, machines being turned off, the tread of feet heading toward the elevators.

Eunice popped her head around the partition. "Another late night, Julia?"

"I just want to finish these book reviews."

"This makes three nights in a row." She pulled her white fake-fur hat more firmly onto her head, then waggled her finger accusingly. "You'll make the rest of us look bad."

Julia smiled. "See you tomorrow." Her smile faded with Eunice's retreating footsteps.

Propping her chin on her hand, she stared at the screen and the letters merged to a white blur. In the craziest way she almost envied Trudi. At the hospital, the day after that surrealistic scene on the river bank, she had thanked Trudi for alerting Martin and asked her where things stood now, for her and Eric.

Trudi had tossed back her blond braids with a snort. "I told him it was the end of the line. Marry me now or I'm moving to Toronto!"

Behind the tough ultimatum, Trudi's fierce loyalty shone through. It had touched her heart. At least the other woman knew exactly what she wanted and was determined to stand by Eric, no matter what.

She could only hope Eric saw it, too. He'd been kept in overnight, for treatment of slight hypothermia, and she had gone to see him, finding him sitting in his hospital bed, haggard and woebegone but calm. After stumbling through another deeply felt apology, he had thanked her profusely for not turning him in.

"I can see I need to make a lot of changes, but Trudi

assures me I can do it. I don't deserve her, but I suppose she must really love me," he murmured.

Just that morning he'd called to tell her he was applying for an opening with a newspaper in nearby Saint Catharines.

"It would be real reporting, not just rewriting press releases like I do here. I'm a little nervous about taking this plunge but . . . but it's what I've always wanted to do."

He had sounded excited and anxious, the words tumbling over each other, but she had put down the phone with a smile. Somehow, she was pretty sure now that he and Trudi would be all right.

Putting her plate of salad down on the end table in the living room, Julia went over to the stereo and flipped through her tapes. She popped one into the tapedeck, sank down onto the old green velvet couch, and picked up her plate.

A slow piano cadence filled the room, then Elton John's wistful tenor. She picked at the salad half-heartedly, not even hungry, though it had been almost nine when she got in from work and slipped gratefully into her fleece jumpsuit.

Tired but restless, she didn't want to watch TV, she didn't want to read—she didn't know what she wanted. Since coming back from Niagara, the home she loved had ceased to be her haven. She just found herself prowling around, feeling troubled and lonely, incapable of settling down to anything.

The phone began to ring, but she ignored it. She didn't feel like talking to anyone right now. Let the answering machine get it. After the fourth ring the tape whirred as the message silently played back, then a beep sounded for the caller to respond.

There was a slight pause and then a soft, achingly familiar voice. "Hello, Julia . . ."

In one movement she dived across the couch and grabbed up the phone. "Martin . . . Hi," she gasped, breathless with surprise, her heart racing against her ribs.

"Oh . . . you're there." His husky voice filled her with inexpressible longing.

"Yes." She clutched the receiver tightly in her hand as if afraid he'd disappear at the other end.

He paused for a moment. "How are you?"

She closed her eyes, letting the caressing sound of his voice wash over her. "Fine . . ." Her voice cracked and trailed off into a long silence. "Martin?" Was he still there?

"Yes." Another silence.

"Did you call from the West Coast just to ask me how I'm doing?" The line fell quiet except for the half-heard whispers of other conversations. She thought of the thousands of empty miles between them with despair. So many dark, cold miles. Why did he call?

Eventually he sighed. "I can hear music. What are you listening to?"

"Umm . . . an old tape of Elton John. I haven't played it in ages," she mumbled in confusion. But she was beginning to feel worried. Was he all right? Something was wrong. He didn't sound like himself at all.

"Such sad songs. Are you sad tonight, Julia?" His quiet voice held a note she couldn't quite interpret. Was it wistfulness, longing that she heard there?

She paused for a heartbeat of time. "Yes." Denial was useless, and right now she didn't have the emotional strength to keep up a facade.

"I miss you, you know. I wish I was with you." His tone dropped lower, husky and broken.

She caught her breath at his admission and a lump formed in her throat. "I miss you, too," she said, a catch in her tremulous voice.

He gave another shaky sigh. Did he sound relieved?

No, no, she couldn't read too much into that. "I have to go now. I'll see you soon, okay?"

"Yes . . . all right," she whispered and waited for him to hang up, but he didn't.

Then, very low, so that she almost didn't hear it, he murmured, "Julia? . . . I love you."

Her heart gave a painful lurch and she began to tremble. He said he loved her. Silent tears rolled down her cheeks.

"Julia . . . are you there?" There was a trace of anxiety in his voice. "Did you hear what I said? I said I love you."

She swallowed hard and wiped at the tears in vain. "Yes, Martin, I heard," she choked out.

Oh God, how often had she longed to hear him say those words? But she had to face the bleak truth. Nothing had changed. If anything, it made the situation even more intolerable. The past five days had forced her to confront the harsh reality of loving someone like Martin. And she just couldn't face a life of constant leave-taking. She huddled in the corner of the couch, cradling the phone in despair.

"Julia, why are you crying? Is it because you don't love me too?" His voice was gentle and understanding.

"Oh no, Martin, I do love you, but don't you see it won't work?" she sobbed as scalding tears burned her eyes and spilled down over her cheeks.

"Julia, I have to go now," he said hurriedly. "We'll talk about this when I get back."

The line went dead. In numb disbelief, she stared at the mouthpiece for a moment before slowly hanging up, then buried her face in the chintz throw cushions and burst into tears. There could be no life together for them. Their visions for the future were poles apart.

A knock sounded at the front door and Julia pushed a fist against her mouth to try to control the weeping. She couldn't face anyone right now. The knocking persisted and she stood up, wiping at her eyes with her sleeves.

She paused between the open French doors leading into the tiny hall, caught sight of her face in the hall mirror, and shuddered. Her hair hung in loose, tangled auburn strands around her pale face. Red, swollen eyes stared back at her, ringed with smudged mascara.

She couldn't go to the door looking like this. But the knocking got louder, until she could swear she saw the door vibrating. Julia stared at the solid wood panels, swaying in indecision.

"Julia, let me in! I know you're in there."

She grabbed the brass handle and flung open the door. For a breathless moment she could only stare while the world swung crazily around her.

Martin stood before her, the soft porch light falling on his windblown halo of blond hair. Her heart turned over, then soared in disbelieving joy. With a sob, she launched herself into his arms, uncaring of the snow covering the shoulders of his parka or the freezing cold night air. He was here—that was all that mattered right now.

He clasped her tightly in his arms, lifting her off her feet as he kissed her with a rough urgency she echoed without restraint. Overcome with emotion, she was vaguely aware that he moved them inside and shut the door behind them without his mouth ever leaving hers.

Her toes touched the floor as his kiss became less frantic, slowed and deepened with a burning possessive hunger that made her weak with desire. Her hands twined in his hair, then ran over the cold planes of his face, needing to convince herself he could be real. Finally he took a deep breath and put her gently from him.

"What are you doing here? I thought you were in B.C." She held shaking hands to her burning cheeks.

"My plane got in a couple of hours ago and I came

here straight from the airport." His breathing still ragged, he stroked her shoulders and looked down into her glazed eyes. "I called from the phone booth around the corner. I had to know how you felt about me and I thought you'd put up too many defenses if we were face to face." He swept her into his arms again. "God I've missed you."

She murmured helplessly against his cold, damp parka, "But Martin . . ."

"I know what you're going to say . . ." he interrupted, "but we love each other, Julia. Everything else will work out. We have to find a way to *make* it work." He gripped her arms fiercely.

Julia managed a weak laugh. She had never been so overcome with love before, how could she possibly argue right now? But she tried.

"Martin, we have to be sensible. If we just rush into this, if we let our hearts rule our minds, we could be letting ourselves in for a lot of pain later."

He hugged her tightly. "My sweet, sensible, darling Julia. I'm so happy that you'll always be there to keep me on an even keel." He laughed, a carefree, joyful sound, tore off his coat and boots, and pulled her into the living room.

"Martin, you haven't listened to a word I've said," she protested halfheartedly, while the rest of her just wanted to feast her eyes on the sight of him.

He dropped his knapsack by the couch and sat down, pulling her onto his lap. "Yes, I have. I've given this some serious thought for the past few days, and believe me, my love, it'll work. We'll make it work. Because everything else is unimportant beside our love."

His gaze dropped to her mouth and softened with a flame of pure desire that made her breath catch. With sensual deliberation he slid one hand up her slender thigh and she quivered. Through the soft fleece she felt him lingeringly smooth over the curve of her hip and gently squeeze her rounded flesh, pulling her close for another kiss. A slow, tantalizing kiss that left her hard pressed to remember her objections.

Finally they pulled apart with a sigh. Martin leaned over and opened his knapsack, taking a paper from the side pocket—a fax copy of the mock-up of *Canadian Horizons*' May cover. It was the picture of the excavation site that Dr. McLaughlin at the museum had given her, showing the half-buried skeletons. And underneath ran the title, "The Past Yields Its Secrets." Her title.

"I don't understand." She looked up at him in confusion.

"Don't you, love? You won. Fair and square."

Her eyes widened in astonishment. Much as she had wanted to win, she'd never forgotten the stiff competition. "I can't believe it."

"Congratulations, darling." His eyes held hers, full of loving warmth. "You've done a really good job and I'm proud of you."

Her heart soared with joy and she took a deep breath. "Oh, Martin, you don't know how much it means to me to hear you say that."

"Listen, I've read your article and I think my research will interest you. Between the two of us we may have laid the poor captain's ghost to rest."

"What do you mean?"

"I found out a great deal about your ghostly paramour." He smiled and laid the cover on the end table, then put a hand lightly on her thigh. "My story focused on the intrigue along the Niagara frontier during the war, and I discovered that Fairfax was investigating a spy ring involving double agents from both sides. It looks like Titus Flynn persuaded them to extend their activities to theft and they were counting on the confusion of the expected American invasion to cover their escape.

"We'll never know if Oakshott was involved beforehand, or if he was just a cold-hearted bastard with his eye to the main chance. As for the others he killed, I found a paper hidden in the captain's diary with the names of the officers he suspected. That tells you exactly who those other bodies were. Thanks to young Sarah Balfour, that information never got back to headquarters. And as a result, Fairfax was labeled a deserter, suspected of involvement in the theft."

"But that's terrible. He was a hero, not a traitor. No wonder he haunts the inn."

"Don't feel too badly for the old captain. I've sent all the information to his regiment in England. They're going to officially rewrite his records and clear his name."

"This is incredible, Martin!" She sat up straighter and gripped his shoulders. "How ironic that we were working on almost the same story but approaching it from two different angles. We never did get around to switching diaries, did we? But we still have enough time to pool our research and give Roger a story that will really knock his socks off! We might not put a dent in *Time*'s circulation, but I think between us we've discovered something significant. After all, he wanted us to collaborate."

He looked amused by her enthusiasm, then shook his head. "Forget it. We had a deal and you won fair and square. I'll gladly give you my research, but I won't allow you to do yourself out of the glory of seeing your byline in print for the first time. Enjoy it. Bask in it. Wallow in it. And then get ready for more work. Because I have it stacked up for us."

Julia stared at him, puzzled. Everything was happening much too quickly. Hurricane Martin had blown into town again and she felt as if she were caught up in a whirlwind.

"I have a plan. Do you want to hear it?"

She nodded and Martin settled back on the couch,

snuggling her more comfortably in his arms, one hand curving possessively around her hip.

With a blissful sigh she sank against his broad shoulder and trailed her palm across his chest, loving the feel of his solid warmth beneath the red sweater. At this point she was ready to go along with anything he might have in mind.

"I've cut a deal with Roger, and from now on we work as a team. Of course, he balked a bit at having to pay accommodations for two. Our expenses at the George didn't thrill him. But I told him the solution was simple. We'll share a room from now on." He gave her a bright smile, as if his glib answer had taken care of all their problems.

"Oh, you did," Julia said faintly, bemused by his officiousness and slowly reddening at the thought of what Roger would think. "Martin, how could you?"

That last night at the George had been wonderful, but did he have to go telling the whole office that they had slept together?

"Well, I didn't see any problem with that. We *are* going to be married, after all," he decreed blithely and kissed the end of her nose. Julia gasped and shook her head, bewildered by the speed with which he was throwing all this at her.

"But what does that mean, you want me to travel with you?"

She got up off his lap and moved over on the couch. She loved him, she wanted him, she wanted to be with him, but she still needed to know what he expected of her. And what she could expect of him.

Martin moved over and captured her hand. "We wouldn't be traveling all the time, and we'd have a permanent home to come back to." He glanced around her small living room. "That is . . . if you want me."

For the first time since she'd known him, she saw complete uncertainty clouding his blue eyes. And suddenly everything fell clearly into place. She loved him, and without him she'd be desperately unhappy. It was that simple.

This was how her mother must have felt. She might have cherished a fantasy of settling down in a rose-covered cottage, but Liz Bennett was so in love with her husband she wouldn't have dreamed of changing her life if it meant being without him. And suddenly Julia realized that through all the difficulties of her childhood she'd always drawn strength from her parents' close, loving relationship. The kind she wanted with Martin.

She smiled, leaned over, and softly kissed him. "But I thought you weren't interested in a mortgage and heating bills and all the headaches that go with them," she reminded him, needing to be absolutely sure he was thinking in terms of forever.

"I wasn't, before I realized I was in love with you and how important you'd be to my continued happiness."

He thought of the lonely plane ride out to the West Coast, missing her already, wishing he had woken her up that morning and made love to her again. Right then he knew that everything had changed. She filled a need in him he hadn't even known existed, and now he didn't even want to contemplate life without her.

"I never had a reason to settle down before. Now I do. And when we have children . . . we'll cross that bridge when we come to it."

He looked into her face and smiled back at the happiness shining out of her violet eyes. The future had never looked more wonderful.

"When do we go on our first assignment?" She wrapped herself around him with a blissful sigh and brushed her cheek against his.

"As soon as we get married, and since our first assignment begins in two weeks, I think we'd better get a move on, don't you?" he murmured against her lips.

With a happy nod she sighed, surrendering to the seductive little kisses he placed on the corners of her mouth. But there was one more thing she had to know.

"By the way, I have a bone to pick with you," she breathed.

"Oh really?" He brushed his lips over hers, making her almost faint with yearning, but she couldn't let go just yet.

"How could you leave like that, without even saying good-bye? Especially after what happened the night before." Her voice dropped and Martin drew back a fraction. She caught the sensual amusement in the curve of his mouth and looked up at him from under her lashes, shyly provocative. "And speaking of the night before . . ."

"Yes . . . what about it?" He pushed the hair off her neck and began nuzzling her throat distractingly.

Julia squirmed with pleasure. "Did you enjoy it?" Her voice cracked and she cleared her throat.

He raised his head and lifted her chin, forcing her to look at him. "I left you a note . . ."

"Huh . . . some note." She gave him an arch look. "It was about as personal as an interoffice memo."

He shrugged with a sheepish smile. "I hated to leave like that, but you were sleeping so peacefully and I had a plane to catch. And I knew I'd be seeing you soon anyway." A wicked, mischievous smile spread over his face. "And I did enjoy it. Very much. You don't know what it cost me to restrain myself from waking you up. Or not waking you up." His voice was soft and knowing. "But I knew that after what you'd been through in the last couple of days you needed your rest. Besides that, there were a few things I had to get straight in my own head.

"It had been made forcibly clear to me that my feelings toward you had changed somewhere along the way. When Trudi told me you were in danger . . ." a violent shudder went through him. "You'll never know the cold, unreasoning fear I felt. And the rage . . . God, if he'd hurt you, I think I could have killed him."

He sighed. "I don't go off the deep end like that very often, and I was beginning to suspect that I might be in love with you." He smiled at his wry understatement. "You have to understand I needed to think about what that could mean. The ramifications for both of us. And there was always the chance you didn't feel the same way."

"But how could you think . . . ?"

He held a finger to her lips to halt her flow of protest. "But four days away from you was enough to convince me that I couldn't be without you."

He trailed the finger slowly over the fullness of her lower lip as she smiled, setting off a sensual tingle Julia found incredibly distracting. "It took you four whole days to realize that?"

"No, it took about four minutes," he grinned, "but four days was the soonest I could get back. Four days . . . and four very long nights." His voice dropped to a husky, seductive tone that made her shiver.

"What?" she teased shakily. "You mean there were no attractive waitresses to flaunt your scar at and regale with stories of feasting on elephant fillet?"

"Oh, hundreds. I had to fight them off with a stick. Unfortunately for me, I couldn't get you off my mind." A slow smile curved his lips as he leisurely traced a finger down her shoulder. "I kept thinking about that first day when I climbed in your bedroom window and saw you standing there dressed only in those absurd little scraps of silk and lace."

His finger descended over the slope of her breast, lingering over the taut peak with tantalizing deliberation. Little shivers of breathtaking, sensually explicit pleasure coursed through her until a soft moan of frustrated desire escaped her lips.

"Imagine my surprise that the ice maiden could set my blood on fire." His smile held a world of erotic suggestion.

Julia felt the heat rising in her cheeks. "I must say, you hid it pretty well." She could hardly catch her breath, trying to feign nonchalance. "You certainly gave me the feeling you were unimpressed."

"Unimpressed? When it was all I could do not to reach out and run my hands over your smooth, perfect skin. Which is exactly what I'm going to do later."

"Later?" she echoed faintly, her heart wildly fluttering at the image he had just painted.

"You don't imagine I'm leaving, do you?" He pulled off his sweater and Julia felt desire surging inside her as her gaze ran lovingly over the strong curve of his shoulders under the black T-shirt, the lean, muscled length of his body, and knew that nothing could keep them apart tonight.

"By the way, about that strange epilogue to your story," he murmured, settling more comfortably into the deep cushions of the couch and pulling her against him. "I thought you didn't believe in ghosts."

She snuggled her back against his chest and rested her head on his broad shoulder. "I thought I didn't believe in ghosts either, but I think I've changed my mind."

"Tell me exactly what happened."

She turned to look up at Martin but saw no skepticism in his face and leaned back against him once more.

"It was on my last morning at the inn. I was packing. It was dull and overcast outside and the room was gloomy. Sort of matched my mood."

He leaned his head down and turned her face until she met his eyes and answered his silent question.

"We had that wonderful night and then you were gone. And suddenly I realized how empty my life would be when you'd be gone for good." With a soft groan he gathered her close and his lips found hers in a gentle kiss that more than made up for all those tears she had shed.

"Go on."

His husky voice, combined with the heady promise of his warm mouth, didn't make it any easier to recapture her train of thought.

"So you were a little distracted," he prompted.

"Just a little. Anyway, as I was getting some stuff out of the dresser, I looked up and saw *him* reflected in the mirror. He was standing behind me, a young man with dark wavy hair, wearing a navy jacket with gold braid and epaulets."

"But wouldn't he have worn red?" Martin murmured into her hair.

"No. I asked Amy and she said that was just the infantry. The officers often wore navy or green."

"Then what happened?"

"Nothing. I turned around and there was no one there. Surely I couldn't have imagined him. He seemed so real. He had a smile on his face. A peaceful, gentle smile. I never felt a moment of fear, just wonderment." She sat up and turned to him. "Oh, Martin, do you really think it could have been Captain Fairfax?"

Martin smiled into her eyes. "I'd like to think it was him. And I'd like to think it was his way of thanking you for finally telling his story. And if it was, then perhaps his spirit will really be at rest now and he'll no longer feel the need to haunt the George."

Julia laughed. "Oh, I hope not. What will Amy do without the captain? There won't be any more ghost stories around the fire."

"I doubt that'll stop Amy. Besides, I like to think that the captain is off on another quest."

"What do you mean?"

"Here, I have something to show you," he murmured. Settling into the deep cushions of the couch once again, he pulled her back against him and took a folded piece of paper from the pocket of his jeans. Mystified, Julia opened a photocopy of what looked like an old letter, judging by the spidery copperplate writing. Then she saw the signature, *Frederick,* and realized it was a letter from the captain to his wife.

"I found it concealed in the diary with the other document." Martin smiled at her. "And I have to confess that I planned to use it as emotional blackmail, in case I had trouble convincing you that we belonged together."

Julia looked up at him with an arch smile and then, snuggling closer into his arms, began reading the letter. It opened *My darling Elizabeth* and ended with the words, *This war must end soon and then we will be together. Nothing can ever keep us apart.*

The last words blurred as her eyes filled with tears and she felt a painful lump in her throat. "I do so hope the captain found his Elizabeth."

Martin curved a strong hand around her cheek and lifted her face to his. "So you see, my love, it just goes to show. What we've found is too precious to throw away. Most people only have a ghost of a chance of finding true, abiding love. We've been lucky, Julia."

She gazed up into his eyes, and the love she saw there filled her with a happiness and contentment she'd never known before. And she knew then that as long as she was with Martin, she would always be home.

SHARE THE FUN . . .
SHARE YOUR NEW-FOUND TREASURE!!

You don't want to let your new books out of your sight? That's okay. Your friends can get their own. Order below.

No. 117 HOT COPY by Rachel Vincer
Surely Kate was over her teenage crush on superstar Myles Hunter!

No. 146 PRIM AND IMPROPER by Rachel Vincer
Julia couldn't make Martin understand there could be no truce—no way!

No. 55 A FOREVER MAN by Sally Falcon
Max is trouble and Sandi wants no part of him. She *must* resist!

No. 56 A QUESTION OF VIRTUE by Carolyn Davidson
Neither Sara nor Cal can ignore their almost magical attraction.

No. 57 BACK IN HIS ARMS by Becky Barker
Fate takes over when Tara shows up on Rand's doorstep again.

No. 59 13 DAYS OF LUCK by Lacey Dancer
Author Pippa Weldon finds her real-life hero in Joshua Luck.

No. 60 SARA'S ANGEL by Sharon Sala
Sara *must* get to Hawk. He's the only one who can help.

No. 61 HOME FIELD ADVANTAGE by Janice Bartlett
Marian shows John there is more to life than just professional sports.

No. 62 FOR SERVICES RENDERED by Ann Patrick
Nick's life is in perfect order until he meets Claire!

No. 63 WHERE THERE'S A WILL by Leanne Banks
Chelsea goes toe-to-toe with her new, unhappy business partner.

No. 64 YESTERDAY'S FANTASY by Pamela Macaluso
Melissa always had a crush on Morgan. Maybe dreams do come true!

No. 65 TO CATCH A LORELEI by Phyllis Houseman
Lorelei sets a trap for Daniel but gets caught in it herself.

No. 66 BACK OF BEYOND by Shirley Faye
Dani and Jesse are forced to face their true feelings for each other.

No. 67 CRYSTAL CLEAR by Cay David
Max could be the end of all Chrystal's dreams . . . or just the beginning!

No. 68 PROMISE OF PARADISE by Karen Lawton Barrett
Gabriel is surprised to find that Eden's beauty is not just skin deep.

No. 69 OCEAN OF DREAMS by Patricia Hagan
Is Jenny just another shipboard romance to Officer Kirk Moen?

No. 70 SUNDAY KIND OF LOVE by Lois Faye Dyer
Trace literally sweeps beautiful, ebony-haired Lily off her feet.

No. 71 ISLAND SECRETS by Darcy Rice
Chad has the power to take away Tucker's hard-earned independence.

No. 72 COMING HOME by Janis Reams Hudson
Clint always loved Lacey. Now Fate has given them another chance.

No. 73 KING'S RANSOM by Sharon Sala
Jesse was always like King's little sister. When did it all change?

No. 74 A MAN WORTH LOVING by Karen Rose Smith
Nate's middle name is 'freedom' . . . that is, until Shara comes along.

No. 75 RAINBOWS & LOVE SONGS by Catherine Sellers
Dan has more than one problem. One of them is named Kacy!

No. 76 ALWAYS ANNIE by Patty Copeland
Annie is down-to-earth and real . . . and Ted's never met anyone like her.

No. 77 FLIGHT OF THE SWAN by Lacey Dancer
Rich had decided to swear off romance for good until Christiana.

Meteor Publishing Corporation
Dept. 593, P. O. Box 41820, Philadelphia, PA 19101-9828

Please send the books I've indicated below. Check or money order (U.S. Dollars only)—no cash, stamps or C.O.D.s (PA residents, add 6% sales tax). I am enclosing $2.95 plus 75¢ handling fee for *each* book ordered.

Total Amount Enclosed: $__________.

___ No. 117	___ No. 60	___ No. 66	___ No. 72
___ No. 146	___ No. 61	___ No. 67	___ No. 73
___ No. 55	___ No. 62	___ No. 68	___ No. 74
___ No. 56	___ No. 63	___ No. 69	___ No. 75
___ No. 57	___ No. 64	___ No. 70	___ No. 76
___ No. 59	___ No. 65	___ No. 71	___ No. 77

Please Print:
Name ______________________________
Address ____________________ Apt. No. ______
City/State ____________________ Zip ______

Allow four to six weeks for delivery. Quantities limited.